P9-DWG-981

WE INTERRUPT
THIS SEMESTER . . .

BOOKS BY ELLEN CONFORD

Dreams of Victory

Felicia the Critic

Me and the Terrible Two

The Luck of Pokey Bloom

Dear Lovey Hart, I Am Desperate

The Alfred G. Graebner Memorial High School
Handbook of Rules and Regulations

And This Is Laura

Hail, Hail Camp Timberwood

Anything for a Friend

Impossible Possum
(*Illustrated by Rosemary Wells*)

Just the Thing for Geraldine
(*Illustrated by John Larrecq*)

Eugene the Brave
(*Illustrated by John Larrecq*)

WE INTERRUPT THIS SEMESTER FOR AN IMPORTANT BULLETIN

by Ellen Conford

Little, Brown and Company
BOSTON   TORONTO

COPYRIGHT © 1979 BY ELLEN CONFORD

FIRST EDITION

Library of Congress Cataloging in Publication Data

Conford, Ellen.
We interrupt this semester for an important bulletin.

Summary: Hoping to impress Chip, editor of the high
school paper, Carrie takes up investigative reporting
and soon finds herself in hot water.
[1. Reporters and reporting—Fiction. 2. Journalism
—Fiction] I. Title.
PZ7.C7593We   [Fic]   79–9133
ISBN 0–316–15309–5

BP

Published simultaneously in Canada
by Little, Brown & Company (Canada) Limit

PRINTED IN THE UNITED STATES OF AMERICA

. . . FOR AN
IMPORTANT BULLETIN

{I}

"All right, could you hold it down, please? Would you listen to me, staff?"

Chip Custer, editor of the *Lincoln Log,* rapped on a table for attention.

"Is anybody listening to me?"

Actually, nobody was. Except me. And I'd listen to anything Chip had to say. Even looking at him when he wasn't saying anything was rewarding.

It was the first day of school, and not the best time to call a meeting of the staff of the *Log,* our high-school paper. Everyone in the room — except me — was discussing schedules and teachers, exchanging complaints, and seemed morbidly preoccupied with the need to run home and cover their textbooks.

Bob Teal (Boys' Sports) and Jessie Krause (Girls' Sports) were in a heated debate right behind me. Cindy Wren, circulation manager, was demonstrating something or other to Peter Kaplan on her pocket calculator. Peter was new, as were several others in the room we used for the *Log* office. He was a freshman and looked very eager and expectant.

I didn't pay much attention to him or to the dull roar around me. I just gazed at Chip, watching him get more and more irritated, and thinking how attractive he was when he was angry.

His dark eyes seemed to get even darker and more intense and he folded his arms tightly across his chest. He surveyed his noisy staff with a look of disdain that would have curdled their blood — if they had noticed it.

Unfortunately, none of them did.

"WILL YOU GUYS SHUT UP?"

I jumped a little in my seat. I'd never heard Chip scream like that. I didn't like it. He was attractive when he was angry, but I didn't think there was anything attractive about hysterical.

It did the trick though. The chattering subsided and there was some seat shifting and shuffling as people turned to look at him.

"Thank you very much," he said sarcastically. "Now that I have your attention, I'd like to welcome you all to the first staff meeting of the *Lincoln Log*. Those of you who are new to the *Log*, we're really glad to have you

4

with us. But you'd better be prepared — you're going to *work, work, work* —"

"We're going to fight, fight, fight," added Bob Teal, "and we're going to *win, win, win*."

Chip glared at him. "Thank you, Bob. That was Bob Teal, our Boys' Sports editor, giving you his impression of —"

Jessie Krause jumped up. "Listen, Chip, while we're on the subject of sports —"

"We weren't," Chip began, but Jessie plunged right on.

"I don't think there should be a Boys' Sports editor and a Girls' Sports editor. I think there should just be a Sports editor."

"Jessie," Chip said, "it's too big a job for one person. Too many games go on at the same time. You can't be in three places at once."

"Well, I don't want to be Girls' Sports editor. Girls' sports are nowhere in this school. They don't get half the attention boys' sports do and it's demeaning —"

"Jessie, *please*." Chip was looking a little dazed. "Could we just get organized first and later I'll —"

"But this is part of getting organized," Jessie insisted.

"All right, Jessie, but we're going to get organized in an organized way." Jessie looked puzzled. For that matter, so did Chip, as if he hadn't understood exactly what it was he'd said. But she sat down, still muttering under her breath, and Chip went on.

"First, many of you know that Mr. Gross, who's been adviser to the *Log* for years, retired."

I knew. And I was sorry. I'd really liked Mr. Gross last

5

year. He was a reassuring kind of teacher to have around. I fondly recalled his gray hair and his never-lit pipe and his gentle advice and instruction.

"So we have a new adviser. He's new at Lincoln too. His name is Mr. Thatcher. He's teaching the journalism course, so some of you who are in the class may have met him already." Chip looked around the room and then toward the door. "He should be here any minute," he added, almost apologetically.

"In the meantime, let's get right down to work." Chip began to call out staff assignments, which we'd hammered out over the summer. Most of the big editorial jobs went to kids who had been on the paper before and who had told Chip the positions they wanted.

I was the Features editor, which was really something I could be proud of, since I was only a sophomore and all the other kids who had editorial positions were juniors and seniors. But I had started working on the *Log* last year and had done a pretty good job as "Lovey Hart," the advice columnist — at least, up until the last part of the year, when the entire school population nearly put out a contract on me. I had also written the "Lighter Side of Lincoln" column, so Chip figured I was experienced enough to be an editor.

Besides . . . I was going with Chip.

"Carrie," said Jessie, tapping me on the shoulder, "you can talk to him, can't you? You can see my point."

"Sure," I said. "But you talk fine, Jessie. I think you have a good argument."

6

Bob Teal snorted. "I think she wants to be Sports editor."

"Well, why not?" snapped Jessie. "Why does the Sports editor have to be a *boy?*"

"But, see, there isn't just one Sports editor," I said.

"Well, there should be," Jessie retorted.

"I have a feeling we're going around in circles," I said. "Anyway, it has nothing to do with me — I mean, I can't —"

"Hey, there's Mr. Thatcher," said Bob.

I looked toward the door. Chip was talking to a short man with dark, curly hair and a really terrific tan. If that was Mr. Thatcher, he was awfully young to be a teacher, I thought. He wore gray-tinted glasses and Frye boots and had a stack of books under one arm. A blue nylon windbreaker was slung over his shoulder.

"He looks like a student," whispered Jessie.

"Maybe it's because he's so short," Bob said.

"Maybe it's because he's so *young*," I murmured.

Chip and Mr. Thatcher walked to the center of the room. Everyone was quiet now; Chip didn't have to do a thing to get the staff to pay attention. Mr. Thatcher had us all staring.

"I want you to meet our new adviser, Mr. Thatcher," Chip announced. "He's going to say a few words to you about his concept of the school newspaper, and how he sees his role as our adviser." Chip moved over to one side.

Mr. Thatcher sat himself on the front table and

crossed his leg so his right ankle rested on his left knee. "First of all, we're all equals here. I mean, there's no hierarchy."

Jessie snorted.

"Tell that to your boyfriend the dictator," she muttered to me.

"I expect to learn a lot more from you than you will from me about the workings of a student newspaper. After all, I'm a stranger here myself." He flashed an appealing, toothpaste-white grin.

I couldn't help smiling back.

"He's *cute*," Jessie whispered, her voice all softness now.

"You're too tall for him," Bob snickered.

"What difference does height make?" she hissed.

"Shh!"

But he *was* cute. And *I* wasn't too tall for him.

What am I thinking of? I have Chip — the only boy I ever wanted. I had just spent two glorious months with him — when he wasn't wrapping hamburgers at McDonald's — two golden, romantic months, a summer to remember. . . . Sun-baked days at the beach, soft, moonlit nights at the drive-in movie, free hamburgers when the manager wasn't looking. . . . Here I was, going with the boy I had loved from afar all last year, and I was feeling myself go all melty over Mr. Thatcher, who was, after all, just another pretty face.

Get hold of yourself, Caroline Wasserman, I told myself sternly. You are reacting like a fickle adolescent with unbalanced glands. Well, I replied to myself, I *am* an adolescent. And how do I know what condition my glands are in? And Chip is the only boy I ever went with, so I certainly am not fickle.

Besides, I get the same feeling looking at Burt Reynolds.

That brought me back to reality.

"So what I'm saying is," Mr. Thatcher went on, "that I believe in the First Amendment — and I believe that the First Amendment does not only apply to adults, but to kids too. And I respect your right to print what you want, and I hope to be the kind of adviser who trusts you enough to leave the production of the *Lincoln Log* entirely in your hands. I don't believe in censorship, and I don't believe you'd find working on the paper much of a learning experience if I checked up on you every step of the way."

He looked for a moment as if he were expecting a round of applause. But no one clapped. It is possible that very few people in the room knew what the First Amendment was.

"And I mean it when I say there are no hierarchies here. I don't want to come on like an authority figure. No more of this 'Mr. Thatcher' business. We *are* all equals. You can call me Mark."

This caused a little stir. Everyone seemed to be a lot more impressed about calling a teacher by his first name than by having their constitutional rights read to them.

"Does that mean we call you Mark in class too?" asked Bob.

Mr. Thatcher — I mean, Mark — looked a little uncomfortable.

"Uh, well, I think in class you better call me Mr. Thatcher. Not everyone in the class is on the paper. . . ." His voice trailed off. "They wouldn't understand," he added.

"I thought we were all equal," Cindy muttered.

"Only some of us," Bob whispered. "We're special, so we get to be equal."

"That doesn't make sense," Cindy said in a low voice.

"Some people are more equal than others," I said. "Remember *Animal Farm?*" We had to read that in ninth grade.

"It didn't make sense then either," Cindy replied.

"That's the whole point," I said.

"I still think he's cute," hissed Jessie.

"Well, if we're all equals," I said, "go get him." Everyone was buzzing again. Mr. Thatcher had finished his little speech and waved good-bye as he left. I was kind of surprised that he wasn't going to stay for the rest of the meeting, but I guess that he meant what he said about leaving the paper entirely in our hands.

Chip returned to the business of handing out assignments and "getting organized," and Jessie and Bob practically raced each other up to the front of the room to argue with Chip about the Sports editor problem.

I just sat at my desk, waiting for the meeting to be over. Then Chip would drive me home and we would be alone and he would hold my hand at red lights. . . . I was burning with impatience to get out of there.

I mean, I had all these stupid *books* to cover.

✳   ✳   ✳

Chip drove me home at last, but didn't hold my hand once.

It was practically five o'clock. Getting the argument between Bob and Jessie straightened out had taken almost half an hour, and you'd think Chip would have had enough *Log* talk for one day.

But not Chip. He sat in his little bucket seat and I sat in mine, the stick shift on the floor separating us, and he talked business.

"Don't you think I did the right thing? Making Jessie assistant editor? I think she wanted the title more than anything. And Bob really wanted to stay with sports, otherwise I would have made him assistant editor. He has seniority anyway. Jessie will still be here next year, and he won't, so he should get what he wants. It was reasonable, don't you think?"

"I think so," I agreed.

We came to a red light. Chip rested his hand lightly on the stick shift. I sighed. It was probably as unnerving to him as it was to me, this business of going together. Although he was a senior, I was the first girl he'd ever been interested in, and I guess he was still uncertain about things. I wasn't any help, I know. After all, I was only a sophomore, and he was the first boy I had ever gone with. Even though it was three months now, I still felt a little shy when I was alone with him like this, and I was pretty sure he sometimes felt shy himself. He seemed so secure on the surface — last year, before we had anything but a "business" relationship, he was practically the picture of self-confidence. And, most of the time he still was. Especially as editor of the *Log*.

But when it came to us — well, maybe we were both sort of testing the water with our toes before plunging bravely in. Sitting in my bucket seat, watching his hand grip the stick shift, I was sure that my feelings for him were real, and that my response to Mr. Thatcher's pearly smile was simply what you might call your automatic Burt Reynolds Reaction.

The light changed. "And we hardly got into the investigative reporting thing at all," Chip was saying. "I really wanted to get people started thinking about that."

"Next time," I said, trying to be comforting. "Organization always takes so long. I think you did great just getting everybody's positions set up."

We turned onto my block and Chip pulled into our driveway.

He didn't turn the motor off.

"Come in for a few minutes?" I asked hopefully.

"It's late," he said, shaking his head. "Almost dinner-time."

He leaned over and kissed me lightly. I closed my eyes, sighed happily, and waited for another kiss. Of course there would be another kiss. Surely Chip wanted to kiss me again. Nothing happened.

I opened my eyes. Chip scowled and gestured toward a pile of books on the back seat. "And besides, I have to get all those damn books covered."

❧{ II }❧

⌘ "Did you ever hear of anything duller?" I asked Claudia. " 'New Faces at Lincoln.' I don't know how Chip could do this to me."

"You're the Features editor, aren't you?" Claudia said. "That's a feature, isn't it?"

"Oh, stop being so logical," I snapped. "That's one of your most annoying faults."

"I didn't know being logical was a fault." Claudia grinned. "Anyway, you said yourself you needed experience doing interviews. So Chip is really doing you a favor."

"Some favor. Interviewing new teachers. No one's going to read that."

"So who do you want to interview? Burt Reynolds?"

I sighed deeply. "*Yes.*"

"You have to start small."

"That's not necessarily true, Claudia," said Terry, my other best friend. "She started out big last year, when she did the 'Dear Lovey Hart' column."

"Yeah, and look how it turned out," Claudia said.

I groaned. "*Please* don't remind me."

"Carrie wasn't ready for Lovey Hart," Claudia went on. "That's why all hell broke loose."

"The *school* wasn't ready for Lovey Hart," I corrected. "And I asked you not to remind me. What's past is past."

"Those who ignore history are condemned to repeat it," Claudia quoted.

"History is bunk," I quoted back.

"Who will you interview?" asked Terry.

"You mean, you're actually interested?" I asked.

"Well . . . not interested so much as curious," Terry admitted.

"Mr. Sachs, my biology teacher."

"Oh, Carrie, what a good idea!" Terry cried. "He's gorgeous."

"Is he interesting?" asked Claudia.

"Who knows?" I said. "I haven't done the interview yet."

"Who cares!" sighed Terry.

Mr. Sachs was tacking up a picture when I entered his room the next afternoon.

"My my," I said brightly, "an amoeba."

"Paramecium," he corrected. "You have not been doing your homework."

He tacked up another picture right next to it. "This," he said, "is an amoeba."

"Oh, right." I barely glanced at the picture. It was very hard to concentrate on one-celled organisms with Mr. Sachs barely five feet away from me.

What was the matter with me? Last week Mr. Thatcher just walked into the *Log* office and smiled, and for several whole minutes I forgot that Chip existed. Now here I was with the incredibly gorgeous Mr. Sachs — who, by the way, was practically the exact opposite of Mr. Thatcher in appearance, being tall and blond and fair-skinned — and I found myself gulping like a fish on dry land.

You're really very shallow, Caroline J. Wasserman, I told myself. This is just *another* pretty face. Looks aren't everything. It's character that counts. Personality. Intellect. All that stuff.

"You're here for the interview?" Mr. Sachs sat down on his desk. I nodded.

"Why don't you sit down?" He motioned toward the student desk in front of him. "I've never been interviewed before."

"That makes two of us," I said nervously. "I've never *interviewed* anybody before." I sat down where he'd pointed and pulled a piece of paper out of my notebook. He was awfully close to me. Seated at the desk in front of him, I had to look up to see his face. If I kept my eyes level, I stared straight at his stomach.

15

I swallowed hard. I will *not* look at his stomach.

"I have a list of questions here. . . ." My voice came out almost in a squeak. "Would you tell me your first name, please?"

"Ralph."

Oh dear. Reluctantly I wrote it down next to the question. Ralph is such a blah name.

"Can you tell me something about your previous teaching experience?"

"I don't have any. This is my first job. In teaching, I mean. I did graduate work for my doctorate but I still have to write my dissertation. Then I'd like to go into college teaching."

I wrote fast, hoping I was getting everything right, and hoping that he wouldn't get his dissertation finished too soon.

"What's your dissertation going to be about?"

"Dimorphic development of transplanted juvenile gonads in mosquitoes."

I dropped my pen. I reached down to pick it up, and stared at him. He was smiling.

"Really? How interesting." I didn't have the slightest idea what dimorphic meant, let alone the rest. "Well, we'll just say you're working on your dissertation."

"Good idea."

"What do you do in your spare time?" I asked. "Do you have any hobbies?"

"I like tennis."

I wrote "tennis" and waited. But he didn't add anything else.

I don't play tennis.

"Do you like music?"

"Oh, yes. I like to listen to music."

Me too. "What's your favorite kind?"

"Uh — easy listening, semiclassical, that sort of music."

"Semiclassical? What is that, exactly?"

"Oh, you know — the score from *The Sound of Music*, things like that."

"Right." I cleared my throat. "Are you — uh — married? Children?"

"No to both." I barely managed not to yell, "Yay!"

"How do you like it here at Lincoln?"

"It's fine, so far. I've only been here a week."

"Well." I stuck the piece of paper back in my notebook. "That seems to be all the questions I had to ask you." I wished I could think up some more, but my mind was a blank. I really didn't want to end the interview yet. I racked my brains for another question, anything to stretch out my time with Mr. Sachs, but no sudden inspiration was forthcoming.

He stood up. So did I.

"Well, thank you very much," I said. "We'll send a photographer to take your picture if that's okay with you."

"Sure."

Barely twelve inches separated us. My heart began to pound wildly. I was sure if he listened hard he could hear it.

I grabbed my notebook and said, "Well, good-bye," in a voice that I hoped was loud enough to drown out the tom-toms in my chest. I fled from the room hearing his voice behind me: "Don't forget to study your one-celled organisms!"

NEW FACES AT LINCOLN
by Carrie Wasserman

<u>Ralph</u> <u>Sachs</u>

Mr. Sachs is new to Lincoln this year. In fact, he's new to teaching. Fresh out of graduate school and working towards his Ph.D., Mr. Sachs hopes to teach in college someday. (Lincoln's loss will be Harvard's gain!)

He enjoys tennis and semiclassical music. Although he has only been here a short time, he finds life at Lincoln "fine."

"That's it?" Chip asked, handing me back the interview I had just typed up.

"What do you mean, that's it? Doesn't he sound interesting?"

Chip looked at me curiously. "Are you kidding, Carrie? Did you write it like this on purpose to prove to me the column would be dull? I know you didn't want to do the column in the first place, but even so —"

"Chip! He's a very interesting man. I don't think he's dull."

"But that doesn't come across, Carrie."

"Well, I can't imagine why not," I said coldly. I had typed up the interview right after I left Mr. Sachs, rush-

18

ing to the *Log* office to get it on paper while our meeting was still fresh in my mind — and while his extreme gorgeousness was still exerting its disturbing effect on my nervous system. How could anyone think Mr. Sachs was *dull?*

"Besides," I added, "you saw the list of questions I made. I asked him the questions. Those are his answers."

Chip looked impatient. "I didn't think those were the *only* questions you were going to ask. I expected you to come up with something a little . . . stimulating."

I was stimulated, I nearly burst out — but didn't. Chip would probably not have appreciated the remark.

"Read it out loud, Carrie."

"Why?" I asked, puzzled.

"Just read it out loud and hear how it sounds."

Bob Teal was sitting at one of the typewriters. The clacking of the keys had stopped. He was listening to every word.

"All right," I snapped. "Mr. Sachs is new to Lincoln . . ."

I read the whole thing out loud. After the first two sentences, Bob began typing again.

"There," Chip said when I'd finished. "You see what I mean?"

"No."

"Carrie, I don't believe this. Either you're —" He stopped suddenly and just stared at me. Angrily, I stared back. What was the matter with him?

He took a deep breath. "Look, I'm sorry but I don't want to print this. At least, not in this form. Why don't you take it home and work on it some more? Pep it up a little. Get some life into it."

I glared at him. He put his hand on my arm. "Hey, Carrie, don't be mad." His fingers tightened on my arm and he pulled me close to him. I looked down at the floor. "Come on, Carrie." His voice was coaxing. "You're such a good writer. I didn't mean to hurt your feelings."

But my feelings were so confused I didn't even know if they were hurt. How could I be in love with Chip and have these crazy reactions to Mr. Thatcher and Mr. Sachs? Here, now, with Chip's fingers wrapped around my arm, I felt only Chip existed and he was all I wanted. But five minutes ago I was furious at him, and half an hour ago, I was having to force myself not to look at Mr. Sachs's stomach.

Bob had stopped typing again.

"All right," I muttered. "I'll work on it."

Chip put his arm around my shoulders and gave me a little hug. "You're not mad at me anymore?" he asked teasingly.

I leaned against him and sighed. I didn't know *what* I was anymore.

I got a ride home with Terry and Marty, since Chip was staying late to do some more work. Marty had just finished football practice and Terry had just finished waiting for Marty.

I'd known Marty since kindergarten and we'd been really good friends up until last year. But just friends. Marty was bland, uncomplicated, broad-shouldered, and totally dedicated to football. We were still friends — but now that he was going with Terry it really wasn't the same.

I read them the interview with Mr. Sachs. "Now, don't you think he sounds interesting?" I asked, when I'd finished reading.

"It's not very long, is it?" commented Marty.

"It's quality that counts, not quantity," I said sharply.

"That's true," Marty agreed.

"What do you think, Terry?"

Terry giggled. "I think if you have a picture of him over the article, it doesn't matter what the article says."

"We're going to have a picture — but that's not the point. Do you or don't you think this is an interesting interview?"

We stopped for a red light. Marty turned to look at Terry. "What do you mean, if there's a picture over it?"

Terry snuggled close to him. "Oh, Marty, you don't have to be jealous." She giggled again.

"I'm not jealous. I just don't know what you mean about the picture." That was Marty for you. He probably *didn't* know what Terry meant.

The light changed to green. Terry was still snuggling.

"Hey, gang?" I said. "About the interview? Terry?"

Horns began to blare behind us. Marty put his arm around Terry.

"The light's green," I pointed out. Marty kissed Terry on the nose.

"You can go now," I said loudly. Terry kissed Marty on the chin.

"The light is . . . oh, forget it." I gave up. They probably couldn't hear me anyway, what with all that honking behind us.

"Dad, what do you know about Ralph Sachs?"

"Who's Ralph Sachs?" he asked.

"You know, the new bio teacher. My teacher."

"I don't know anything about him," he said. "And even if I did, you know I couldn't tell you."

My father is the head guidance counselor at Lincoln. This could be a sticky situation, so we have this rule that, in school, we pretend that we don't know each other, and neither of us gets involved in the other person's activities. But we weren't in school now.

"Chip says I ought to pep up my interview with him. I can't imagine why, but he says it's dull. I thought you might give me a little inside information — you know, nothing confidential or anything like that."

"Even if I knew anything about him — which I don't — I couldn't tell you. And even if I did — which I wouldn't — you couldn't print it, because he'd know he didn't tell you the information himself."

I sighed. "That's very logical," I said. "But it doesn't help me a bit."

"You want to show me the interview? Maybe it's just a matter of style."

"Yeah, sure." I went to get the interview from my notebook. My mother and Jen were sprawled across my parents' bed, watching the news.

"Mom, come and listen to this, will you? I'm reading an interview to Dad, and I want your opinion."

"All right." She followed me downstairs, and Jen followed her.

"I'll give you my opinion too," my sister said generously.

"I didn't exactly ask for your opinion," I pointed out.

"That's okay."

Jen had been a real pain last year and caused me a lot of trouble, but now that she was twelve she was going through a completely different phase. She was still mostly a child, of course, but she was experimenting with being a woman (I think that's the way my father put it) and we were trying to be careful about her feelings. She did not, however, always exercise the same concern for our feelings.

I read it out loud. When I was finished, Jen said, "*Yawn.*"

"What do you know about it?" I retorted.

My father wouldn't look me straight in the eye. "I don't think," he began hesitantly, "that it's just a matter of style."

"No, substance is more like it." My mother nodded.

"What do you mean?"

She gave me a rueful little smile. "There isn't any."

"*Mom!*"

"I'm sorry, Carrie. It's just that I know you're a good writer. I've seen you do so much better."

"Forget it!" I snarled. "Forget I asked. Nobody in this

house is a writer anyway. I shouldn't have expected you to know what's good."

"You don't have to be a professional writer," Jen said snootily, "to know what's *bad*."

I stormed up to my room and tore my interview into tiny pieces. Mr. Sachs wasn't dull. I mean, one look at him and you knew he had to be fascinating. *I* was fascinated. How could anyone who made my blood rush through my veins in such a violent fashion be dull? And if he was so fascinating, how come I wasn't able to get that across in my article?

Maybe interviews just aren't my forte, I told myself. What other explanation could there be?

⟨ III ⟩

"Investigative reporting," Chip said forcefully, pounding on the table. "That's the thing. How do newspapers win awards?"

He looked around the *Log* office, waiting for an answer. No one responded.

"Investigative reporting!" I shouted back, trying to sound enthusiastic. Someone had to, and even if I felt silly, a certain loyalty to Chip required me to back him up.

"Right!"

"What are we going to investigate?" asked Jessie.

"Whatever smells rotten. We're going to dig up scandal and corruption and expose it."

"The cafeteria always smells rotten," Cindy said. "Especially at lunchtime."

"Do you really think there's any scandal right here at Lincoln?" Bob asked lazily.

"There *must* be," Chip said. "It stands to reason. We're a big school. Somebody here has to be a crook."

"Gee, I hope so," Peter Kaplan said eagerly. "But where do we start?"

"Well, you were only kidding about the cafeteria, Cindy," Chip said, "but there *is* an awful lot of room for corruption there. For instance, let's say the guy in charge of ordering the food says he's buying a certain grade of meat. What if he buys a lower grade of meat, but charges the school district for the higher grade?"

"And pockets the difference!" Peter shouted.

"Exactly." Chip beamed.

"For all we know," Cindy said, her eyes blazing, "they could be feeding us *horsemeat*."

"That's right," said Jessie. "How do we know what went into those meatballs today?"

"And God knows what they put in the chicken chow mein," Cindy said morbidly.

"What a bunch of crooks!" Peter's voice was outraged.

"Uh, wait a minute," I said. "We don't *know* that anyone did that. Chip was just giving us an example."

"Well, I wouldn't be surprised," Jessie said.

"I wouldn't put it past them," Cindy agreed.

Actually, I wouldn't be surprised either. Claudia and I had often puzzled over how it was possible to make a tuna fish sandwich taste like crunchy glue spread between two household sponges.

"Okay," said Bob. "So we investigate the cafeteria. How do we do that?"

"It doesn't necessarily have to be the cafeteria," Chip said. "What about books? How do they decide which textbooks to buy? Maybe one company is paying someone kickbacks to get them to buy their books. So instead of buying the *best* geometry book, let's say the guy in charge of ordering geometry books buys the one from the company that bribes him."

That wouldn't surprise me either. I was taking geometry this year, and it was a complete mystery to me. Well, no wonder I was doing so poorly. No wonder I couldn't understand how to prove that two isosceles triangles were whatever it was we were supposed to prove they were. How could I be expected to learn geometry with a substandard book? It wasn't going to be *my* fault if I failed geometry.

"Okay," Bob said, "but how do we find out these things? I don't think if we walk up to the head of the cafeteria and ask him right out, he's going to admit he's feeding us horsemeat."

"That's where the digging comes in," said Chip. "The hard-nosed investigating. The detective work."

"The snooping," Jessie added. "The sneaking around."

Chip nodded. "You could put it that way."

"But *how?*" Bob insisted.

"I'm glad you asked me that," Chip said with a proud smile. "We use a cover story. We *say* we're doing an article on one thing, while we're actually looking around for clues for our exposé."

"I don't get it," Peter said.

"You go to the head of the school lunch program," Chip explained. "You say, the *Log* wants to do a whole detailed article about how the program works. How do you feed a thousand kids every day?"

"Very badly," said Jessie.

"You tell them you want to see the whole process, right from the beginning, when they plan what to order. They'll probably be glad someone is finally going to give them some recognition and you'll get a tour and an explanation and maybe a snow job, if they're covering up something. What you have to do is see if it's snowing."

That sounded really exciting! Chip was right. Imagine if we could expose the school lunch program as riddled with graft and corruption, a poisonous stain on the Lincoln banner, a cafeteria headed by a veritable Godfather of Gravy, a Capo of Cole Slaw! The *Log* would certainly get some sort of public-service award — maybe even a Pulitzer Prize. I mean, what could be more of a public service than ripping the lid off a lunchroom that was hazardous to kids' health?

"So we'll start with the cafeteria?" Chip asked.

"YES!" we all shouted. The staff was full of enthusiasm now. After all, every one of us had eaten there — if you could call it eating.

Chip assigned himself and Jessie to interview Mr. Fell, who ran the lunch program for the whole district. I was really disappointed. I sort of automatically expected that since Chip and I were going together, we would be crusading reporters together. I didn't know if I would have been so enthusiastic about investigative reporting if I had known that Chip would be doing the investigating with Jessie.

Not that I was jealous, or anything like that. Jessie was two inches taller than Chip and was the captain of the girls' basketball team. She was equally devoted to the sport and to Donald Pflug, the center of the boys' basketball team.

But still . . .

And then, to top it all off, when Chip handed out the rest of the assignments:

"Carrie, we'll need another 'New Faces at Lincoln' column."

"Oh, Chip, no! You didn't like the first one I did."

"That's why I want you to do another one," he said patiently. "Because we can't use the first one. And besides, you've got to learn to do interviews sometime. It'll be good for you."

"So would eating my spinach," I grumbled. He was beginning to sound like a father figure, stern but kindly, knowing better than I did what was in my best interest.

"Look, Chip, I'm the Feature editor, right? That makes me an editor, right? Then why can't I assign this feature to one of the staff, instead of having to do it myself? And why can't I pick something I'd really like to do? That's one of the privileges of being an editor, right?"

"But Carrie, you haven't come up with any other features yet, so you haven't got anything to assign. And we haven't decided on what stories we're going to do, so the only other thing in the features line is 'Innovations in the Language Lab,' and you'd have to interview Mrs. Mazzi for that anyway."

"Dull," I muttered. "Dull, dull, dull."

"I know," sighed Chip. "We always seem to have the same problem. If we don't get something really hot in the way of a scandal, we're going to be right back where we started from last year — with no one even looking at the *Log*."

"Well, 'Innovations in the Language Lab' and 'New Faces at Lincoln' certainly won't help any."

"Your 'Lighter Side of Lincoln' column was pretty popular," Chip reminded me. "You can do that again. But right now —"

"I know, I know," I grumbled. "Scour the classrooms, looking for a fresh new face."

I gave Peter Kaplan, who was eager for an assignment, the language lab story, which promised to be even more boring — if that were possible — than another new teacher interview.

Especially when I realized that I didn't *have* to scour the classrooms for a new face. Happiness, as Dorothy discovered in *The Wizard of Oz*, was right in my own backyard — so to speak.

Mark Thatcher. What could be more appropriate for the first issue of the *Log* than an interview with its new adviser? And having heard Mr. Thatcher's remarks at the staff meeting, I felt sure that he'd have plenty of interesting things to say.

Besides, I felt I had really learned something from my first 'New Faces' interview with Mr. Sachs. It wasn't enough to just report word for word what your interviewee said — you had to make him *come to life* on paper. It wasn't that Mr. Sachs was dull. My interview was dull. Though *I* had found Mr. Sachs fascinating, I hadn't conveyed my feelings to the reader. I hadn't put anything of *myself* into the article; I'd just coldly presented facts. And let's face it. Facts are boring.

Tracking down Mr. Thatcher was just slightly easier than finding the lost continent of Atlantis. He never came to *Log* meetings, and no matter how quickly I sped from my homeroom to his after the last bell, he was always already gone. Finally, after days of fruitless attempts at making contact, I left a note in his mailbox begging him to wait in his homeroom for me that afternoon so I could interview him.

At three o'clock I raced to Room 208, fully expecting that

a) He had not gotten my note, or

b) He had gotten my note but ignored it, or

c) He made it a practice never to grant interviews, or

d) He actually didn't exist, and the day he appeared in the *Log* office he was simply a figment of our imagination, created by mass hypnosis.

Much to my surprise, he was in his room, erasing something from the chalkboard. His back was to the door. He was barely an inch taller than I am, and he almost had to stand on tiptoes to reach the top of the board. I thought that was rather endearing. I stood in the doorway a moment, just watching him erase, sort of enjoying the view.

I could have stood there for quite some time, a silent admirer, but Mr. Thatcher finished erasing, and when he turned around, he saw me.

"Oh, hi there. Are you the girl who left me the note?"

"Yes," I said weakly. The front view of Mr. Thatcher's head was even more scenic than the back.

"Well, come in, then. I'm very flattered that you want to interview me."

He smiled his dazzling white smile.

Interview? What interview?

Oh, *that* interview. I sighed. I seemed to be doing an awful lot of sighing these days. Chip probably wouldn't like it if he knew how much sighing I was doing when he wasn't around. Especially since his absence was not the cause of my sighs.

You are being silly again, Caroline J. Wasserman. You are thinking silly thoughts and dreaming foolish dreams. Remember how impatient you were with Terry when she had a crush on her French teacher last year? So why are you standing here gazing at Mr. Thatcher (*Mark*) and waiting for him to tell you that the moment he spotted you at the *Log* meeting he found himself madly, hopelessly, desperately in love?

"What's your name again?" Mr. Thatcher asked. "Carly?"

So much for foolish dreams. Down to business, Carly.

"No, Carrie. Caroline Wasserman."

32

"Okay. What do you want to ask me?"

I *want* to ask you to marry me, but since this is strictly business . . .

"Could you tell me something about your newspaper background?"

I whipped out my trusty pen and my little black leather notebook, which I had bought because I thought it made me look professional. None of the Ace Reporters I had ever seen in movies carried looseleaf notebooks around when they were on the trail of a hot scoop. I thought I looked rather dashing with my new tools of my trade.

"Don't you have a tape recorder?" asked Mr. Thatcher.

"A tape recorder?" I repeated blankly. "Why?"

"It makes interviewing much easier. You don't have to rush to write down what your subject says, which means you don't make mistakes or misquote him. Unless you take shorthand?"

I shook my head. I don't take shorthand. I just abbreviate a lot.

"All the professionals are using them now."

Deflated, I looked at my little black notebook with new contempt. On the top line of the first page I wrote, *"Get hold of tape recorder."*

NEW FACES AT LINCOLN
by Caroline Wasserman

Mark Thatcher

Looking young enough to be a student, possessing a mind brimming with innovative ideas on every subject from freedom

of speech to organic gardening, Mark
Thatcher breezes through the halls of
Lincoln High like a breath of fresh air
in a musty old attic.

Running his hands through his curly
black hair, propping his feet on the
desk, he explains to a visitor why he
feels so strongly about freedom of the
press.

"You remember what George Washington
said — about if he had a choice between
a government with no newspapers and newspapers with no government? He said he'd
rather have newspapers and no government.
That's how I feel. The people's right to
know is the most important right we have
in the Constitution. It must be pro-
tected at all costs."

Suddenly he smiles warmly and the
visitor is dazzled by the pearly perfection of his teeth. "That's why I'm so
strongly committed to a laissez-faire
approach as adviser to you people on the
Log. Censorship of the press is the
first step towards dictatorship. You
wouldn't want to live under a dictatorship, would you?"

Not waiting for a reply, Mr. Thatcher,
his thoughts moving faster than a speeding bullet, begins to talk about his
past.

"I was a journalism major at Colum-
bia," he says. "You really get the
groundwork there, but when you graduate,
you find that the only way you're going

34

to learn what journalism is and where
it's at is by on-the-job experience. So
for a year I worked on a paper in
Shawnee Mission, Kansas."

Coming back east, Mr. Thatcher found
that the fierce competition for jobs on
major newspapers and the steady decrease
in the actual number of newspapers being
published left him, though highly qualified, dedicated, hardworking and experienced, temporarily unemployed.

"So I came here," he tells his visitor,
idealism shining in his deep, brown
eyes, "thinking that the next best
thing to actually working on a newspaper was teaching young people, the
journalists of tomorrow, to be the best
they can be."

Welcome to Lincoln High, Mr. Thatcher!
The Shawnee Mission <u>Herald</u> <u>Intelli-</u>
<u>gencer</u>'s loss is our gain!

"Uh, Carrie," Chip began, frowning at the typed copy
he had just read, "who is this 'visitor' you keep talking
about?"

"Me, of course. I thought that was obvious — yet subtle,
you know? I mean, saying 'he explained to this reporter'
is so trite and pretentious."

"Why do you have to mention a visitor at all?"

"You wanted a peppier interview," I said irritably.
"This is the New Journalism. Where the reporter becomes
part of the story."

"I don't know if the *Log* is ready for the New Journalism, Carrie," Chip said. "At least, not the way you do it."

"Oh, thanks a lot!" I was furious. "You said you wanted —"

"Hey, hey, don't get excited. This is really much better than the Sachs interview. *Much* better. Lively. Good quotes. A little controversial."

That's better, I thought. That's more like it.

"The thing is . . ."

"*Yes?*"

Chip took a deep breath. "Well, there are a couple of things. You're not part of the story at all — I mean, you're just there, you don't do anything but listen, so there's no need to refer to a 'visitor.' "

"*Yes?*" I was getting angry again.

"And all this stuff about his curly hair and dazzling smile — is that really relevant?"

It is to *me*, I wanted to retort, but thought better of it.

"I think it helps," I said coldly, "to give the reader a word picture of the man they're reading about."

"But we'll have a photo of him," Chip reminded me. "They'll see what he looks like."

"And if we ask him very nicely," Bob Teal said, "maybe he'll give us a dazzling smile for the camera." Bob finished reading the interview and handed it to Cindy, who had been listening with interest to our discussion.

I scowled at him.

"And his idealism is your opinion, Carrie," Chip pointed out. "To me it just sounds like he took up teaching because he couldn't get a job on a newspaper. That's not idealism — that's desperation."

"Of *course* it's my opinion," I agreed. "In the New Journalism the reporter is entitled to have a reaction to her subject."

"I don't think George Washington said that about the government and the press," Cindy broke in. "Are you sure Mr. Thatcher was talking about George Washington?"

I had been writing awfully fast during the interview with Mr. Thatcher because he had been talking awfully fast (almost as if to prove to me I really *ought* to get a tape recorder), so it was possible I had made one or two teeny mistakes. I checked my little black notebook and found the scrawl of the quote I had attributed to George Washington. It read: "Gov't or papers? Papers. MT agrees."

There was no mention of George Washington. When you don't take shorthand you have to rely a lot on your memory. But my memory was pretty good, and I'd typed up the interview just moments after I'd left Mr. Thatcher.

"I'm pretty sure it was Jefferson," said Cindy.

"Well, yeah, Jefferson, Washington, one of the Founding Fathers, I'm sure of that."

"There's nothing like accuracy," Bob said sarcastically.

"One little mistake," I grumbled. "And it might not even be a mistake. Maybe Mr. Thatcher *said* Washington. Maybe *he* made the mistake."

Chip seemed doubtful. "There's no 'people's right to know' in the Constitution either, Carrie. Did he say it was in the Constitution?"

I checked my notes. "Ppl's rt. to no mst. imp. rt. in cnt. Prtct. at all csts."

"He must have said it. It's here in my notes."

Chip looked disturbed. "If we print it that way, he's going to sound stupid. I mean, *I* know it's wrong and I'm only a student. How's that going to make *him* look?"

I certainly didn't want to make Mr. Thatcher look stupid. That was the furthest thing from my mind. And he wasn't stupid, he was brilliant. He had a mind that seethed with intellectual thoughts, and he was extremely adorable and the last thing I wanted was for him to hate me for making him look ignorant in the school paper.

I turned to the first page in my notebook and drew two bold lines under *"Get hold of tape recorder."*

"Let's just leave that out," I said. "The part about it being in the Constitution."

"Good idea." Chip took a pencil and crossed it out. "Actually, Carrie, with a little editing this is going to be very good." He crossed out some more things.

"A *little* editing?" I peered over his shoulder. "What are you doing?" He was drawing lines through all the best parts.

Out went the curly black hair, out went the "visitor," out went the pearly teeth, the dazzling smile, the idealistic eyes. Out went the "thoughts faster than a speeding bullet." Out went highly qualified, hardworking, dedicated.

"Oh, Chip!" I was raging. "You ruined it! You said you wanted something lively, and now you take out everything lively." I snatched my interview from him. *"Will you stop crossing out things?"*

"I'm finished," he said mildly.

38

I turned away from him. I waited for him to apologize, for him to ask me not to be angry. I would accept his apology, of course, but coldly. And I would still be angry at him. Didn't I have good reason? After all, he hit me right in my creative temperament, and that *hurts*.

But Chip didn't apologize. He just walked over to where Jessie was working on a story, leaned over the back of her chair, and began talking to her in low tones.

There was a distinct possibility that I might burst into tears on the spot — but just then Bob said, "Hey, Carrie, you know what occurred to me? Both the interviews you've done so far have been with good-looking men. Is that just a coincidence, or what?" He practically leered at me.

"There aren't that many new teachers," I said defensively.

Chip looked over at us, then quickly lowered his head and apparently became absorbed in Jessie's story.

"It seems pretty suspicious to me," Bob said, grinning.

"You have a suspicious nature," I said. "And if you must know," I went on, loud enough for Chip to hear, "it was no coincidence."

I turned and stalked grandly out of the office, my haughty exit slightly marred by a collision with Peter Kaplan, who was just coming in.

"Carrie, I got the interview with Mrs. Mazzi. Would you check it over and see if it's okay?"

"According to *some* people," I said coldly, "I am the *last* person to ask about interviews." I pushed my way past him.

Chip would certainly not be driving me home today. Well, I had two perfectly good legs. I could walk. I also had two perfectly good eyes. I could cry.

I might even, I thought, giving my locker door a savage kick, start on that last part *right now*.

{IV}

I lay on Claudia's bed, my chin hanging over the edge, and stared at the floor. I groaned hopelessly.

Terry hunched on the rug, elbows resting on her knees, hands cupping her face. From time to time she emitted a quiet little whimper.

Claudia looked from one to the other of us. "This is terrific," she said. "Misery in stereo. Wall-to-wall gloom. Why don't you two work up an act and hire yourselves out to entertain at funerals?"

"It isn't funny," said Terry. "You just don't understand. I have a problem and you make jokes."

She has a problem, I thought scornfully. *She* sinks into a profound despair if she has to sew a button on a shirt and doesn't have the right color thread. Terry is such an extremist. When she's up, no one in the world ever experienced such joy. And when she's down, no one — but no one — has ever suffered such intolerable anguish. The smallest thing can set her off in either direction — and she stays, either in ecstasy or in agony, until some new and equally insignificant incident propels her in the opposite direction.

She has a problem? Humph. I snorted.

Now *I*, on the other hand —

"Well I do," Terry insisted. "Wouldn't you be upset if you were going with someone who loved a football more than you?"

"That's tragic, Terry," I said sarcastically. "That's really tragic."

"How do you think it feels," Terry asked, "to play second fiddle to a piece of horsehide?"

"Pigskin," corrected Claudia, "but let it pass, let it pass." She grinned at her own joke.

"Do you have any idea what 'being in training' means?" Terry went on. "Do you know all the things you're not allowed to do when you're in training? We can't go out Friday night because there's a game Saturday. Saturday night he's so tired from the game that we have to go to the early show at the movies and he falls asleep there anyway. And he has to be in bed by ten o'clock every night. And I'm sick of going to Burger King and having him say, 'I'll have it my way. *Raw.*' It's disgusting."

"He certainly takes training seriously," Claudia commented.

"A lot more seriously than he takes me," said Terry. "If it were another girl, I could fight that. But it's just . . . *demeaning* to know that he loves a dumb game more than he loves me."

"Football season will be over in November," Claudia said consolingly. "Then he won't be in training anymore and —"

"But Claude, don't you see? I'll still know that I'm not the most important thing in the world to him. What kind of a meaningful relationship can we have if he cares more about a bunch of jocks than he does about me?"

"Listen, Terry," I said, "every girl who goes with a football player has the same problem. You're not unique, you know. There are twenty-five other guys on the team in training too. You think you're the only one who —"

"I happen to feel things very deeply," Terry said. "*Some* people may not be as sensitive as I am."

I rolled over on the bed and sat up. "You just can't let anyone else have a problem, right, Terry? You won't admit that anyone else —"

"Girls, girls," Claudia broke in. "Let's not argue about which one has a better reason to commit suicide. Actually, Carrie, I don't think your situation is so much different from Terry's."

"How can you say that?" I demanded. "The difference is night and day."

"I don't think so," Claudia said. "Because what you're really unhappy about is that Chip seems to be more concerned with putting out a good paper than with your feelings. And that's what made you mad."

I stared at her. I had never thought of it that way. But she was right. When Chip criticized my interviews, he wasn't doing it because he was critical of *me*. He was just doing what he thought was in the best interests of the *Log*. And what bothered me, I guess, was that he wouldn't compromise his standards of perfection — and Chip was a perfectionist, I knew — just because we happened to be going together. So, to break it down to its simplest terms, I played second fiddle to the *Log*, just as Terry complained she played second fiddle to a football.

"I guess you're right," I admitted. "But the thing is, Terry is still going with Marty, while I —"

"But the magic isn't there," Terry cut in vehemently. "Knowing that you aren't —"

"Oh, shut up!" I growled. "It's my turn."

"*Well!*" Terry turned her back on me to face the bust of Beethoven that glowered on Claudia's desk.

"While *I*," I continued stubbornly, "have hardly spoken to Chip all week."

"Well, whose fault is that?" asked Claudia. "You're the one that got huffy in the first place."

"But I had a good reason. At least," I added, "I thought I did at the time. And he never tried to apologize or anything."

"Because he didn't have anything to apologize for," Claudia said.

"If he really cared about me, wouldn't he have said something? At least, ask me what was wrong?"

"Carrie, he's as insecure as you are. I mean, you've practically said so yourself. He doesn't know how to handle this. In fact, he's probably very hurt and confused."

She was right. I was sure she was right. I thought over the events of the past week, the way I had treated — or not treated, to put it more exactly — Chip, and the occasional bewildered looks he shot in my direction. While I had been nursing my own hurt, I had been too self-absorbed to consider his point of view. I knew he was sometimes shy with me. I knew that he was inexperienced with romance, yet I had ignored all that.

"What should I do?" I asked.

"As I see it," Claudia began, "you have two choices. You can go in on Monday and pretend nothing happened, acting like you're going with him again, just as you were before. Or you can explain how hurt you were and why you were mad at him, but now you're not because you thought it over and you understand why he's the way he is, and you hope he understands why you are the way you are."

"That's a little complicated," I said, "but I think I see what you mean."

"At least," Terry said coldly, "there's a solution to *your* problem, Carrie."

Suddenly I felt great. So great, in fact, seeing that there *was* a solution to my problem, that my irritation with Terry completely dissolved.

"All right, Ter," I said, my voice full of sympathy, "tell us about how the magic isn't there anymore."

* * *

45

I couldn't wait until Monday. That was too long. So the moment I got home, I ran upstairs to my room and called Chip.

"Chip?"

"Carrie?" He sounded hesitant. Confused. Unsure of himself. Puzzled. *Adorable.*

"Oh, Chip, I've been — I mean — I wanted to tell you —" This was a lot harder than I thought. I knew what I wanted to tell him, but didn't know how. I mean, I was as new at this game as Chip, and almost two years younger to boot. Maybe making up comes easy if you've had a lot of practice, but this was a first for me.

"Well, I know I've been acting kind of — uh — actually, the thing is —"

"I'm sorry I hurt your feelings about those interviews," Chip broke in, his voice soft and deep.

"But you were right, Chip. I'm sorry I was so touchy about a little criticism. I understand now, I really do."

"No, Carrie, I should have been more tactful. I just didn't think."

"Oh, Chip." I felt a glorious, overwhelming relief . . . the sun suddenly breaking through a week of icy drizzle in my soul. Just saying his name gave me a little thrill, and picturing him as he must be right now, holding the phone close to his ear, murmuring into the mouthpiece —

"Carrie? You want to do something tonight?"

"Oh, Chip."

"Here's what we have so far," said Chip. We sat around the long table in the *Log* office, Cindy, Jessie, Peter, Bob, and I. Chip riffled through scraps of paper on which he'd collected notes about his investigation of the school lunch program.

"Different companies submit bids to the school district for different items. Say, one company will specialize in hamburger and hot-dog rolls, bread, et cetera. Mr. Fell says if the products are of comparable quality, he'll take the lowest bid. BUT. On things like chopped meat he doesn't *have* to take the lowest bid. He says there you have to take into consideration things like percentage of fat to lean, protein content per ounce —"

"The pedigree of the horse," Cindy added.

Peter and I giggled appreciatively.

"Anyway," Chip went on, "in things where he doesn't have to take the food from the lowest bidder, but makes decisions about the quality of the food he's going to buy, there might be a lot of room for double-dealing. Jessie, what was your impression of what he told us?"

Jessie shrugged. "He really didn't tell us anything that sounded suspicious. I mean, much as I hate to admit it, I didn't spot anything shady."

"Neither did I," Chip agreed, "but I didn't expect to. After all, if he *is* doing anything illegal, it's not going to show up on the account books or the orders, because those are examined every year by the school district. And if he's got records that look okay to experienced accountants, we're certainly not going to spot anything the experts didn't."

"Then where do we go from here?" Cindy asked.

Chip looked disheartened. "I'm not sure. If only we

had someone who knew how to tap a telephone . . ." He looked around hopefully. "I don't suppose any of you —"

We all shook our heads. "I have trouble changing the batteries in my radio," said Bob.

"Is that legal?" I asked doubtfully. "Tapping a phone?"

"It may be illegal, Carrie," Chip said, "but we'd be doing it for a good reason. An exposé of the lunch program would be a *public service.* Anyway, it doesn't matter, since no one knows how. See, I'm sure none of the underhanded dealings ever get into the records. These have to be private agreements he makes with each of the companies he does regular business with. And it would only be verbal — nothing would ever be put down on paper. That way you have no evidence."

"Then it's a dead end," Peter said bleakly.

"Unless we can come up with another idea, I don't see where else we can go with it. I was hoping one of you could think of something."

We all looked around at each other, exchanging blank, helpless glances. Chip spread his arms in defeat. He looked so disappointed it made me want to cry.

"We might come up with something yet, Chip," I said, trying to sound encouraging. "A new angle, or something. Maybe if we all think about it for a few days . . . after all, right on the spur of the moment we can't think of anything, but who knows?"

Chip nodded glumly. "Maybe." He didn't sound convinced.

{V}

"Hah they-ah. Is this the *Log* office?"

I looked up from my typewriter. Standing in the doorway, leaning lazily against the frame, was the most beautiful girl I had ever seen in my life. Bob Teal, who was working at the desk next to mine, inhaled so sharply I could hear the breath whistle in his lungs.

No wonder. She was about five foot four and had a waist the size of a Barbie doll's. Above and below the waist her body's curves were in perfect proportion and nicely accentuated by a snug French T-shirt of dusty rose and a flowered challis skirt that clung to her hips before it flowed to a soft swirl around her knees.

Her hair was the color of wheat and she was the only

person I had ever seen whose skin fitted the old "peaches and cream" cliché. Her features were so perfect and even that you would think God had been working with a micrometer to place them exactly right. While she had the same set of sensory equipment — eyes, nose, mouth — as the rest of us ordinary mortals, *her* set was obviously the deluxe model.

Bob leaped from his desk, knocking over his chair, and raced toward this vision, probably expecting her to vanish before he reached her. But she didn't vanish. She stayed just where she was, leaning in the doorway, as if the M-G-M photographer was about to shoot her publicity stills.

I reached over and set Bob's chair back on its legs and it was at that very moment that I knew I hated her.

"This is indeed the *Log* office," Bob said grandly, panting only a little. Cindy Wren, the one other staff member in the room, shot me a wry smile. I'd never heard Bob use the word "indeed" before.

"What can I do for you?"

"Ah'm new he-ah, and it said ovah the PA that you were lookin' fo' people to help on the pay-pah, and it's too late to try out fo' cheeahleadin' . . ."

Cheerleading's gain is our loss, I thought grimly.

"Of course you're new," said Bob, leading her into the room, "because I don't remember seeing you before and if I had, I certainly would remember. Our humble office is honored by your presence."

Cindy looked like she wanted to throw up.

"We'll need some information before you can work

on the *Log*," Bob went on smoothly. "Name? Marital status? Phone number?"

She giggled softly. There was not, as I hoped there would be, a large, ugly gap between her front teeth. I should have known. There is no such word as "semiperfect."

"Ah'm Prudie Tuckerman," she said. "Ah'm single, of coahse."

Bob exhaled with dramatic force. "Thank you," he said, gazing heavenward. "*Thank you.*"

Cindy and I exchanged looks of pure disgust.

"You don't really need mah phone numbah, do you?"

"Oh, I do, I *do*," said Bob urgently.

She giggled again. "It's unlisted," she said, honey in her voice. Bob waited, but she didn't tell him the number.

Just then Chip burst into the room, waving a sheet of paper.

"Listen to this!" he shouted. "I just —" He screeched to a halt in front of Prudie Tuckerman. For a moment he just stood there, staring. Then he gulped. I know he gulped, because I saw his Adam's apple move.

"Well. Hi," said Chip. He sounded breathless. Of course, he *had* been running.

"Hah they-ah."

"Do you want to work on the *Log?*" Chip asked incredulously.

"It was too late to try out for cheerleading," Bob said.

"If you want me," Prudie said with a little smile. Her tone sounded modest, but that smile revealed that she knew perfectly well what Chip's response would be.

"I'm the editor in chief of the *Log*. Chip Custer."

"Editor in chief," echoed Prudie, with admiration. She said it the way I would say "Burt Reynolds."

She was leaning back against the table now, her palms flat on the surface, her rear end resting lightly against the edge.

She was a great little leaner.

Cindy Wren looked at me, cocked her head to one side, and raised her eyebrows, as if to say, "Are you going to sit there and let this happen?"

I sent her a look of utter helplessness. What can I do? I thought back at her.

She stood up determinedly and beckoned for me to follow. She strode to the front of the room and planted herself between Chip and Bob, waiting pointedly to be introduced.

I stayed in my seat. Eventually Chip would notice me. Wouldn't he?

"This is our circulation manager," Chip said, finally aware that there was somebody else in the room besides Prudie. "Uh — uh —" Incredibly, Chip seemed to be struggling to remember Cindy's name!

Mindy Wren, I thought bitterly. And I'm Carly Wasserman.

"Hah they-ah. Ah'm Prudie Tuckerman."

If she said "Hah they-ah" one more time I was going to run amok. I may, I thought, run amok anyway. It is just about time to run amok, if for no other reason than to distract Chip from Scarlett O'Tuckerman. And if I broke a few windows in the process of running amok, at least we could clear the air of the thick cloud of magnolias and molasses that seemed to be hanging over the room like an inversion layer of smog.

"Chip," I called, my voice sharper than I meant it to be. "What was that paper you were yelling about?"

He spared me a fleeting glance. "Sure, sure," he said absently. He turned back to Prudie. "Prudie," he said softly. He gestured vaguely in my direction. "That's our Features editor, uh —"

Carly Wasserman, you fickle fink.

At last I stood up and marched over to the group. I took Chip's hand in mine possessively, something I had never done before in front of other people. But Little Miss Grits had better know right from the start that Chip is mine.

I smiled insincerely at her. She looked amused, as if she knew exactly what I was doing and why. I had this chilling realization that to Prudie Tuckerman there was no such thing as "Mine." Unless it was hers. It would make no difference to Prudie if Chip happened to be going with me, if she wanted him for herself. In fact, clinging to Chip's limp hand I had a sudden premonition that it would make no difference to Chip either.

I dropped his hand. I cleared my throat nervously.

"Chip, that paper you were waving around?"

At last Chip dragged his eyes from Prudie and looked in my direction. "Oh! I almost forgot!"

I can't imagine why.

"I spent my two free periods in the lunchroom observing," he said. "I thought maybe if I watched the process

53

from the final end, instead of trying to track it down from Mr. Fell's office, I might spot something we'd never find just looking at books and records."

"Did you?" asked Cindy.

"Did I! I have the hottest story since Lincoln was shot!"

"Ooh, how excitin'!" squealed Prudie. She clapped her hands together. "Ah had no ideah workin' on a school pay-pah would be this thrillin'."

You ain't seen nothin' yet, cookie. Just wait till they pick me up for first degree murder.

"What is it, Chip?" Cindy demanded. "What did you find out?"

"Someone," Chip said darkly, "is being bribed by the milk company."

{VI}

What with World War I, the Depression, World War II, Kennedy's assassination, the Vietnam War, and Watergate, it was hard for me to believe that hanky-panky with Happycow Wholesale Dairy Products, Inc., was the biggest story since Lincoln got shot.

However, since none of those stories had broken first in the *Log*, perhaps to us this *was* the Biggie. Chip seemed convinced of that, anyway.

"I even got an informant on the staff," he said proudly.

"Who?" asked Bob.

Chip shook his head. "You know I can't tell you. My informant swore me to secrecy. We'll refer to him or her only as 'Cottage Cheese.' "

Cindy and Prudie burst into a fit of giggles. I had to press my lips together to keep from laughing.

"Does it have to be 'Cottage Cheese'?" Cindy gasped. "I mean, couldn't you have thought of something a little classier?"

Chip looked hurt. "I thought 'Cottage Cheese' was pretty good. Anyway, it's too late to change it now."

"Ah hate cottage cheese," murmured Prudie.

"On the other hand," said Chip, "I don't want to be unreasonable. We could call him — or her — 'Yogurt.' "

Ah hate yogurt.

"Yogurt, cottage cheese, what's the difference?" Bob said impatiently. "The important thing is, how much can he tell us? And do we have to pay him?"

"We don't have to pay a thing," said Chip. "He — assuming it's a he, which you shouldn't assume — is doing it for the good of the school. His conscience is bothering him and he says he can't keep quiet any longer about what he's seeing."

"What is it exactly that he's — assuming he's a he —" Cindy said carefully, "seeing?"

"That the school is being shortchanged by two to three hundred cartons of milk a day. Every delivery is short that amount."

"So maybe the milk company is cheating on the order," Bob said. "Isn't someone checking the deliveries?"

"*Exactly!* And the person checking the deliveries knows perfectly well that the orders are coming in short. And *never reports it.*"

"Which means?" I asked.

"That the school is paying for a certain amount of milk," Cindy began excitedly, "but getting less, and the person who's in cahoots with the dairy is being bribed not to report it. The bribe probably comes out of the extra profits they're making on the milk they don't deliver."

"But how much can that amount to?" Bob asked.

"Plenty," said Cindy. "Even if the school's cost for each container of milk is only ten cents — and it's probably more — that's two hundred to three hundred times ten cents —" She whipped out her calculator and figured quickly — "that's twenty to thirty dollars a day, which is a hundred to a hundred and fifty dollars a week, and if there are forty weeks of school, that's between — *four and six thousand dollars a year!*"

"Even if their inside man only got a third of that," Chip said, "that would be a lot of money to someone who worked in the cafeteria. Their salaries can't be so high that an extra grand or two a year wouldn't mean anything."

"But it's not a lot of money to the dairy," I pointed out. "Why would they do that to make a measly couple of thousand a year?"

"Because we're not the only school they supply," said Chip. "What if they have contracts with *ten* schools?"

"Ohh." I nodded. "That wouldn't be measly anymore."

"So are we going to drop the Fell investigation and just use this?" asked Bob.

"The Fell thing is at a dead end," said Chip. "And that really bothers me, because now that I know about the

57

milk, I'm more convinced than ever that the corruption starts right at the top. If someone is finding it so easy to rip off the school at the bottom level of the program, think of the opportunities the guy in charge of the whole system must have." He shrugged. "But I don't know what to do about it. In the meantime, we have a nice scandal to start off with for our first issue, and if my headline doesn't grab their attention, nothing will."

"You've written the headline already?" asked Bob. "Before you even wrote the story?"

"It just came to me," Chip said dreamily, "as I was coming back here. 'LUNCH PROGRAM RIDDLED WITH CORRUPTION! MILK PAYOFFS LEAD LIST OF LINCOLN SCANDALS!' Then, under that, we have a subhead: *Dairy Company Bribes Just the Tip of the Iceberg.*' "

"Wow!" said Bob.

"One bribe doesn't exactly make the program riddled with corruption," Cindy pointed out. "Where's the rest of the iceberg?"

"That," Chip said proudly, "is exactly what Cottage Cheese is going to find out for us."

When I got home that afternoon, Jen was sitting at the kitchen table, her legs wrapped around the legs of a chair, eating strawberry yogurt.

"Why," I demanded, "are you eating strawberry yogurt?"

"Because the seeds get stuck in my braces when I eat the raspberry kind," she said reasonably.

"I hate yogurt," I muttered.

"So don't eat it." Jen continued to spoon the stuff from the container, rolling her tongue lovingly around each gloppy mouthful.

It was disgusting.

I went up to my room, flung my books on the desk, and threw myself onto my bed, prepared for a good, long sulk.

I had left Chip in the *Log* office, pounding madly away at a typewriter, with Prudie Tuckerman practically draped over his shoulder. I knew I shouldn't have left him alone with her. I'd kept telling myself so all the way home, but I didn't know what else to do. Chip didn't have any assignments for me and the thought of draping myself over his *other* shoulder and watching him type seemed a little ridiculous. No matter how hard I tried I wouldn't be able to compete with Prudie on her level. It just wasn't my style to coo admiringly at Chip and make inane comments like, "Mah, mah, ah nevah saw anyone type so fay-est in mah whole life."

While Chip, that dummy, preened himself like a peacock and typed faster.

I could have stayed and worked on my "Lighter Side of Lincoln" column, but I knew instinctively that as long as Chip was there Prudie would hang around; and when it came time to go home, Prudie would wangle a ride from Chip. That would mean that Chip would have to drop one of us off first . . . either Prudie or me . . . and I just couldn't face the almost certain humiliation when Chip chose between us.

59

No, I couldn't compete with Prudie on her level — in fact, I couldn't compete with her on any level. There was no doubt in my mind that Chip was thoroughly infatuated with that sugarcoated snake, and why not? Poor, naïve, inexperienced Chip. He had no defenses against a Prudie Tuckerman; how could he? He was not used to girls chasing him at all, let alone girls who looked like *her*. I could understand why he was making a slobbering idiot of himself when Prudie dripped honey all over his shoulder and went into ecstasies over his typing ability.

How would *I* feel with Burt Reynolds hanging over *my* shoulder, saying things to me like, "I've always dreamed of meeting someone who could type that fast. . . ."? I could certainly imagine *my* reaction.

Which I proceeded to do, for about five minutes. It was a welcome distraction from the problem at hand, but left me, in the end, more depressed than ever.

Because, let's face it. If *I* had to choose between Burt Reynolds and Chip (I should have such problems) the decision would take about three seconds . . . or as long as it took to tell Chip, "It was great fun but it was just one of those things and I'm off to Hollywood." Therefore, if Chip had to choose between Prudie Perfect and Caroline Commonplace is there any doubt in anyone's mind what his decision would be?

Well, that's that, I told myself briskly. There's no point in brooding anymore. Life must go on.

I am through with men, through with love. I will dedicate myself to my career, starting right now. I will throw myself into my newspaper work with every ounce of talent and energy I possess, instead of frittering away my time with foolish dreams and bittersweet memories.

This would be my destiny: "Carrie Wasserman, Star Reporter."

No, that didn't sound right.

"Caroline Wasserman, Star Reporter."

No, not quite.

"Caroline Jane Wasserman, Star Reporter"?

No.

"C. J. Wasserman." That was it. "C. J. Wasserman, Star Reporter."

"*Exclusive to C. J. Wasserman,*" the bylines would read.

A tape recorder, I thought suddenly. Claudia has a tape recorder! Simultaneously, I remembered Chip's frustration because he could not go further on the investigation of Mr. Fell.

In an incredible flash of inspiration I realized that my career as a star reporter was about to begin.

{VII}

"But Marty," I insisted desperately, "there's *got* to be a way. There just *has* to."

"But there isn't," Marty said. "Not with this kind of equipment. The best you can do is set the timer to turn it on and hope that your victim says something incriminating within forty-five minutes, because that's the longest cassette you've got. Now if you had, say, six recorders and six timers, you could set them to go on in sequence, and get six forty-five-minute tapes."

"Even if we did," I said gloomily, "I doubt that we could hide all that stuff near one telephone."

"I don't know how you expect to hide *one* of these things next to one telephone. First of all, you've got a built-in mike, so the whole recorder has to be near enough to where the guy is talking to pick up his voice. Then you've got to have it plugged into the timer and the timer has to be plugged into an outlet. Now, how are you going to set all that up so it can't be spotted?"

"I don't know," I said, "but I have to. I just *have* to."

"Who is this guy you want to bug?" Marty asked for the third time. "What's so important about him?"

"You know I can't tell you."

"Yeah, you keep saying that. You ask me to help you and I come right over and do my best to help you and you won't even tell me what I'm helping you do."

"You're helping me to get hard evidence against a possible criminal," I sighed. But you're not helping me much, I thought. When I borrowed Claudia's tape recorder to bug Mr. Fell's office, I had not dreamed of all the difficulties that would be involved. I had just pictured myself clutching a cassette full of incriminating conversations to my bosom, sprinting down to the *Log* office and pounding out my story on a typewriter, while Chip phoned the printers and screamed, "STOP THE PRESSES!"

It never occurred to me that there might be a few complications along the way before my career as a star reporter actually got off the ground.

Now here I was, with a great idea, an inspired idea, the very thing that would make my name a legend in the history of student journalism, and Marty was telling me there was no way to make it work.

"How are you going to do it, Carrie?" Marty persisted. "How do you think you're going to get away with it?"

"I don't know. I haven't even seen the office yet. Until I do, I can't tell. But I'll find a way. Believe me, I'll find a way. Now show me how that timer thing works again."

Mr. Fell's office was in Lincoln, along with all the other district offices, in a separate wing on the first floor. For two days, Peter Kaplan and I cased the joint, missing our lunches and arriving late to several classes with breathless explanations. We were trying to find a pattern of lunch hours or coffee breaks or something, when both Mr. Fell and his secretary would be out of the office at the same time.

Peter was thrilled to be in on my investigation, but as a spy he had certain drawbacks. In particular there was the problem of his appearance. He simply was not inconspicuous. He was quite tall and thin, had hair so blond it was nearly white, and he dressed with slightly more flamboyance than Elton John.

He promised to wear something quiet and nondescript for our first scouting mission, but he looked so troubled when he promised that I suspected he was mentally rummaging through his closet wondering if he *owned* anything quiet and nondescript.

He showed up in school the next day wearing a black suit that was too short for him, with a white shirt, a narrow black tie and navy blue Pumas over white sweat socks. He did not exactly blend into the woodwork. He looked like an overgrown albino undertaker ready for a quick jog around the funeral parlor.

"Uh, Peter," I said as we walked down the hall together, "for someone who was supposed to dress inconspicuously, you're certainly attracting a lot of attention."

And he certainly was. People stopped and stared, elbowed their friends, pointed and whispered. The two-headed woman at a circus sideshow never received such attention.

"They're probably surprised to see me dressed so conservatively," Peter said, sounding quite pleased. "Compared to how I usually look."

"That must be it," I muttered. I was about to call off the first spying mission when I figured that if anyone saw Peter dressed like this today, they might never recognize him again when he returned wearing his usual fuchsia and chartreuse flowered shirts. Which I would see to it he would wear from now on.

The next day he arrived in a trench coat and sunglasses, which he wore right through third period. He was quite disappointed when I insisted he stow them in his locker before lurking around Mr. Fell's office.

But for all this trouble, we really didn't accomplish anything useful, except to find out that Mr. Fell and his secretary took separate lunch hours and that during the times we were able to check out the place there was always at least one person there.

"Where do we go from here?" asked Peter on the third day.

I shook my head helplessly. It seemed impossible.

Meanwhile, I had to fend off Claudia's morbid concern for her tape recorder.

"Just another couple of days, Claude. No, nothing's

happened to it. No, I won't put it in my locker. Yes, I know my locker has been condemned by the board of health. No, Jen and her 'little friends' have not touched it. No, I'm not keeping any bad news from you. Did it ever occur to you that you have an unnatural attachment to that thing?"

Finally I decided we had to act. At the very least we had to get into Mr. Fell's office and take a look around. From the pay phone in the front hall, Peter dialed the office. He insisted on putting a handkerchief over the mouthpiece to disguise his voice, as we would be seeing the secretary in person and he didn't want her to recognize him. I pleaded with him to take that stupid handkerchief off the phone, as it was a lunch period and the whole world seemed to be passing through the front hall and it was hard not to notice Peter hunched over the phone, speaking mysteriously into a handkerchief.

But he insisted. It was vital that he not be implicated in anything the least bit illegal, he told me firmly, since he planned to be a veterinarian and the tiniest stain on your record was enough to disqualify you from ministering to our Animal Friends.

"No, Mr. Fell is out to lunch now. He should be back at about one-thirty." Peter held the receiver a bit away from his ear so I could listen too. Oh, we certainly looked inconspicuous.

"All right. I'll call him back then. You might tell him Mr. Smythe called. That's Smythe with a *y*," he added. I jabbed him in the ribs so hard he nearly dropped the phone.

"What's the matter with you?" he demanded.

"Why did you do that? All you had to do was hang up."

"I thought it was a nice touch," he said. "She would have been suspicious if I just hung up."

I sighed. It was not the first time that I wondered why I had asked Peter to help me launch my career as a star reporter.

We strolled casually through the district office wing and stopped in front of Mr. Fell's office.

"You let me do the talking," I whispered. "Don't you say a word. Is that *clear?*"

Peter looked insulted.

I had planned this all out in my head. I really didn't expect to get a chance to plant the tape recorder today, but if we got lucky I might at least have the opportunity to look around Mr. Fell's office for a good place to conceal it. And if we got *really* lucky — who knows?

Mr. Fell's secretary was seated behind a desk in a small outer office, beyond which was an open door that obviously led into Mr. Fell's private office, since NELSON FELL was stenciled on it in gold letters.

The nameplate on the secretary's desk read MRS. CHAVEZ. She looked up as we walked in. "Yes?"

"Could we speak to Mr. Fell, please?" I asked, knowing that he wasn't there.

"I'm sorry, he's out to lunch now. Is there something I can help you with?"

I shook my head. "No, we have to speak to Mr. Fell personally." I pulled Peter to a small leather sofa and we sat down. "We'll wait."

Mrs. Chavez looked a bit irritated. "But he won't be back for half an hour at least."

"That's all right. We don't mind waiting."

"Shouldn't you be in a class now?" she asked suspiciously.

"No. We have free periods."

She shrugged. "Suit yourself." She returned to her typing.

"Now what?" Peter whispered.

"Now we wait."

Having no books with me, as I wanted to be able to move fast if the need arose, I gave the outer office a thorough looking-over. That took about thirty seconds, since there was nothing much to look over except Mrs. Chavez, Mrs. Chavez's desk, and the sofa we were seated on, and I had already looked at them. On the wall opposite us there was a painting of a vase of sunflowers.

Nothing happened. Mrs. Chavez typed. Peter and I sat.

Finally Peter leaned over and whispered in my ear, "Stare at her."

I gave him a dirty look and watched Mrs. Chavez's face to see if she had heard him. The rhythm of her typing didn't change.

Stare at her, for heaven's sake! That was so juvenile. Peter didn't press, but changed his position a little and fixed his gaze steadily on Mrs. Chavez. At first there was no response, but after a few moments she glanced up and missed a beat in her typing.

Quickly she lowered her eyes to the dictation pad next

to her typewriter and began to type even faster, as if making up for the interruption. Peter's lips twitched, but his eyes never left her face. Mrs. Chavez began to shift uncomfortably in her chair.

Suddenly the phone rang. I nearly jumped and so did the secretary. She had to turn from her typewriter sideways to answer it and I could swear she seemed almost relieved as she picked up the receiver.

"Yes. Yes, I can. No, really, it's no trouble at all. I'll bring them right over." She stood up, smoothed down her skirt, and patted her curly, red hair. She went into Mr. Fell's office and returned carrying a cream-colored folder. Ignoring us, she bustled importantly out of the office holding the folder in front of her with both hands, like a shield.

"See, it worked!" Peter gloated.

"Nothing worked. The phone rang. Now look, I'm going in there." I pointed toward Mr. Fell's door. "You stand out here, right by this door, and be the lookout. When you see her coming down the hall, whistle 'Dixie.' "

I jumped up and headed for Mr. Fell's office.

"Does it have to be 'Dixie'? I'm not sure I know it."

"What's the difference?" I hissed. " 'Dixie,' 'Yankee Doodle,' just whistle *something*. And don't let her spot you watching for her. Duck right back in."

I scooted into Mr. Fell's office and nearly broke my shin on his desk. The place was hardly bigger than a broom closet, with just enough room in front of the desk for the door to open and close. There was a window behind the desk and to the left of his chair, squeezed up against the wall in the corner, was a four-drawer file cabinet.

The first thing I looked for was an outlet. He had a lamp on his desk and I followed the cord and found that the outlet was on the wall next to the file. But where to hide the tape recorder and the timer in this cubbyhole?

And then I saw it. I'd seen them so many times in our own classrooms that I would never have looked twice if I hadn't been in a new, tiny room where somehow the heat vent looked different.

I squirmed behind the desk and examined the vent, which ran along the windowsill. There was a ridged metal thing inside, where, I assume, the heat came through. But there was no heat coming up now. It was early October and still quite warm. You could see somewhat through the slats of the vent, but who would look?

Time was wasting. How did you get the metal cover off? It was flush against the windowsill. I looked closer. There were two little metal screws, one on each end of the cover. And one looked loose. A flimsy arrangement, I thought, and then thanked heaven it was.

Why hadn't I brought a screwdriver with me?

Well, who would have figured I needed a screwdriver? I scrabbled through my wallet and came up with a dime. Frantically I began using the edge of it to unscrew the vent.

Hadn't Mrs. Chavez been gone an awfully long time? Hadn't I been in here for an awfully long time? It seemed like forever. Had Peter fallen asleep on watch? Had he become so absorbed in studying the sunflowers in the painting that Mrs. Chavez had returned and he'd never noticed?

No time to check. Just keep at it. One screw came up very easily — the one that had looked loose. I ignored all random thoughts about Mr. Fell having a screw loose and went to work on the other one.

It was a beast. But finally it began to give, and my fingers, practically worn to a nub, twirled the dime around in what seemed a very professional manner until I could lift the screw out.

The cover came right up. I leaned it against the window and grabbed the recorder and the timer from my canvas bag. I stuck the recorder into the vent and set the timer for two o'clock. I checked hastily to make sure that the recorder was plugged into the timer and that the button was set to record. I turned the volume dial all the way up.

I was just ready to close the vent with a sigh of relief when I realized that the timer cord would have to come out of the vent to be plugged into the wall outlet next to the desk.

I nearly groaned out loud. How could he miss *that*? The cord was black, the windowsill white, the vent cover gray. And I wouldn't be able to screw the vent back on flush with the sill if the cord was bulging out from it.

Frantically I tried to think. There were orange and green curtains at the windows. Their hems brushed the sill. If I pulled them over slightly they might cover the cord — or at least some of it. But what if the afternoon sun hit Mr. Fell on the back of the neck each day, and he routinely closed his curtains to lessen the impact? One twitch of that drape and the game would be up.

I couldn't just stand here dithering any longer. I had to do *something*. Hardly able to think straight, I snatched the timer out of the vent, pulled out the optional cord from the tape recorder, and let it start recording. There were batteries in it. I put the timer into my bag and had the vent cover in my hands when I heard a sudden, shrill whistle.

"Da da da dum. Da da da *dum*." That idiot was whistling off key, Beethoven's Fifth Symphony. Nothing he could have picked would have sounded more like an urgent signal. I dropped the vent back into place; there was no time to put the screws in, so I snatched them off the sill and dropped them into my purse. It looked fine even without the screws.

I scrambled out from behind the desk, banging my knee in the process, and hurtled into the outer office. Peter was just loping toward the leather sofa and we nearly collided in our rush to sit down and look as if we hadn't moved since Mrs. Chavez left.

Her face fell as she came back in and saw us still there. She frowned and seemed about to say something. Very showily I looked at my watch.

"I guess we can't wait any more," I said to Peter. "We have a class in a few minutes."

Peter looked at his watch too — only he wasn't wearing one. That did not discourage him, however. "Oh, that's right!" he exclaimed, staring at his naked wrist. "I have industrial arts this period. Metal shop, you know. We're making boxes. Little metal boxes. We're going to learn to do the corners today and I wouldn't want to miss *that*."

Mrs. Chavez gave him a fleeting, distrustful look, but I think she was suspicious about his mental health, not his presence in her office. I practically dragged him out of there, while he chattered on about learning to use an acetylene torch.

"What is the *matter* with you?" I demanded, when we'd put a good hundred feet between us and Mrs. Chavez. I wanted to kill him. Inconspicuous was not exactly Peter's middle name.

"Why must you keep elaborating on things that way?"

Peter cackled. "I was throwing her off the trail," he said. "Using a red herring. I don't take metal shop, I have *wood* shop. She'll never track us down. *Never!*" He cackled again.

Mrs. Chavez wasn't the only one concerned about Peter's mental health. In addition to myself, two teachers and four students, who happened to pass by just as Peter emitted his second mad giggle, looked rather shaken.

But no matter, no matter, I told myself. I had planted the tape recorder, which I had never expected to be able to accomplish today, and the only thing I had to do now was pray that Mr. Fell would get back to his office and say something incriminating within forty-five minutes, before the cassette ran out.

And, of course, that no one would turn up the heat.

73

{VIII}

I had a lot on my mind that afternoon, which is probably why I didn't hear the doorbell. Prudie Tuckerman slinked her way in and out of my thoughts like a gossamer python with Chip, that rat, alternately chasing her and being chased. He hadn't called me in days, and answered me only absently when I spoke to him. When he wasn't huddling with Cottage Cheese, he was spending every afternoon in the *Log* office, acting the part of Big City Editor, with Prudie draped decoratively over his shoulder.

And, I began to realize that getting the tape recorder planted in Mr. Fell's office was only Phase One of Plan A. That is, I had only fought half the battle. How in the world was I going to get the recorder back out again? Provided, of course, that Mr. Fell didn't find it, and that the heat didn't go on tomorrow and melt Claudia's precious plastic Panasonic all over the radiator.

Dimly I became aware of a pounding on my door.

"Carrie?" The door was flung open.

"Oh, hi, Claude." Speak of the devil.

"Didn't you hear me?"

"Lot on my mind. Come on in."

Claudia came in. She looked around carefully, as if she were making an inventory for insurance purposes and then said, "I do not see my tape recorder."

"That is because it is not here."

"Where is it? Not in your desk!"

"No, not in my desk." My desk drawers are in worse shape than my locker.

She clutched her chest dramatically. "Thank God."

"Claudia, I must say I think your devotion to that tape recorder is practically neurotic. I mean, what do you think I'm going to do to it?" Besides letting it melt all over a radiator, I thought morbidly.

"But the thing is, what *are* you doing with it?" She made a broad sweep of her arm around the room. "It's not here. You swore you wouldn't put it in your locker. You promised you wouldn't let Jen play with it — so where is it? I mean, it *is* mine, you know."

"I know, I know. You'd never let me forget that, would you? Look, Claude, you're my best friend, right? Will you just trust me for a couple of more days? Right now consider your recorder on assignment. It's covering a very important story for the Log. If things come out right, your tape recorder might even get a Pulitzer Prize."

Claudia looked extremely suspicious. "Is it dangerous? I mean, why are you so secretive about it?"

"It's not dangerous," I said reassuringly. "It's in a very safe place." As long as they don't turn the heat up. "And I have to keep it quiet. You can understand that. This whole thing is highly confidential. Hey, look, Claude, I'm really feeling rotten, you know? I mean, if you came over here to cross-examine me about your tape recorder, I'm not up to it. You don't know how my life is falling apart."

"Ohh, Carrie." Claude softened. "What's the matter? Is it Chip?"

"What else? Do you happen to know a girl by the name of Prudie Tuckerman?"

"Oh my." Claudia bit her lip. She sighed deeply and shook her head. She looked as if she were in mourning.

"I see you know her," I said bitterly.

"I have," announced Jen, "divided my lips into four sections."

I glanced with irritation at the door of my room. "That should make it easier for you to talk out of both sides of your mouth at once."

"Come on, Carrie, look." She pointed to her lips. "The right upper is section A, the left upper is section B, and so on."

"Yes?" I said impatiently. "Section C and section D. So?"

76

"On each section I have put a different color of lip gloss. Section A is Pearly Peach. Section B is Berry Blush . . ."

"Oh, I get it," I said with amusement. "Which one do I like best?"

"Right." Jen approached my desk and stuck her face under my lamp. "Which one is most suited to my skin type?"

"You have Berry Blush all over your braces," I commented. I examined her plaid lips. "Let's see now . . ."

The phone on my desk rang. Jen grabbed it, hitting her head on my lampshade as she sprang up.

"Yes?" Then rather coolly, "Oh, it's you, Craig." The rest of the conversation went something like: "Yes. No. I'll see. Well . . . maybe. Okay. 'Bye." All in clipped monotone.

She hung up. "That was Craig," she said carelessly.

"So I gathered. You could have," I suggested, with sisterly concern, "sounded a little more — uh — interested. Boys like it when you show an interest in them."

She gave me a blank look. "He asked me to the Eighth Grade Get Acquainted Dance. *He's* interested in *me*."

For a moment I just sat there feeling foolish. "What is this devastating power you've got over men?" I asked at last — only half-sarcastically.

"I don't know," she shrugged.

I thought about Chip, of how he gazed at Prudie Tuckerman like a lovesick bloodhound, while I stood helplessly to one side, watching her yank his leash.

I decided Jen didn't need my sisterly advice.

In fact, maybe I ought to ask her for a few pointers.

The phone rang just as I was getting ready for bed.

I picked it up and for a moment all I heard at the other end were little sniffling sounds.

"Oh, hi, Terry." I'd recognize her sniffle anywhere.

"Carrie?" Sniffle. "I feel just awful."

"I never would have guessed. What's the matter?"

"I broke off with Marty."

"Now, why'd you want to go and do something that drastic? In another month football will be finished and —"

"It wasn't only that." Sniffle sniffle. "It was like I told you the other day. The magic has gone out of our relationship."

"How much magic was there to begin with?" I asked dryly. Having known Marty since I was in kindergarten I would never expect any "magic" from him; he was just "good old Marty."

"I don't know." Terry sighed loudly.

I was getting impatient. I had my own problems, much worse than this. What was so tragic about breaking up with someone you weren't crazy about anyhow? Within a week Terry would be madly in love with another boy and would have forgotten all about Marty.

"Listen, Ter, you don't know what miserable means. You want to know what's really tragic? What's really tragic is when you love someone and *he* breaks off with *you.* That's misery. You want to know about suffering? I'll tell you about suffering. I have never felt so rotten in my whole life as I have this week, but did you know that? No, you didn't. Because you're so wrapped up in your own petty problems you haven't got time to notice anybody else's unhappiness. And besides, I'm trying *not* to show people how lousy I feel. I'm trying to be brave and make the best of things. I don't want people to feel sorry for me. That's the difference between you and me." I paused to take a breath.

"Well," said Terry coldly. "I'm really sorry I burdened you with my *petty* problems, Caroline. I thought you would understand. I certainly will not bother you anymore."

"Terry, for Pete's sake —"

"*Good-bye.*" Click.

I stared at the receiver in disgust, then dropped it back on the hook.

I turned off the desk light and got into bed.

Tired as I was, I couldn't fall asleep. It was not as easy to switch off my mind as it was to switch off a lamp. The *Log* office whirled past my closed eyes, like the cyclone scene in *The Wizard of Oz*. Then I got a picture of a sudden snowstorm ("Unusual weather we're havin'") which required the school janitor to turn on the oil burner, which resulted in Mr. Fell discovering the hideous remains of a melted tape recorder in his heat vent.

In and out of my thoughts flitted Prudie Tuckerman, who kept murmuring things like "Honeychile" to Chip, who responded in much the same way that Claudia's tape

79

recorder did to the sudden surge of steam heat. ("Look! He's melting! Who would have thought such a little girl could —")

But what if I did get the tape recorder back safely tomorrow? And what if there was a recording of Mr. Fell arranging some underhanded deal with the chopped-meat supplier?

How excited Chip would be!

We would huddle together, writing up the exposé that would rock the school to its foundations. Prudie Tuckerman would be forgotten. Chip and I would be too busy with the story of the century for him to pay her any attention. And then . . . and then . . .

Chip would at last turn to me and say, "Carrie, what a fool I've been! How could I have ever thought of anyone but you? We were meant for each other." He would point to our names under the banner headline: *"By C. J. Wasserman and Chip Custer."*

"That's the way it should always be," he'd say. "And not only on the newspaper."

I would laugh prettily. "Well, maybe sometimes it could be, 'By Chip Custer and C. J. Wasserman.'" He would clasp my hand in his and —

Forget it. I wasn't doing this to get Chip back. I was doing this because I had resolved to dedicate my life to my work. The whole point was to channel my energies into something more constructive and worthwhile than men. Here I was wasting my time on romantic fantasies when I should be figuring out how to retrieve Claudia's tape recorder from Mr. Fell's office.

Of course, if in the process of launching my career as a star reporter, Chip just happened to come to his senses and —

Forget Chip!

Sure. And while you're at it, Caroline Jane Wasserman, forget to breathe, too.

╉IX╊

I stumbled out of the house the next morning in a state of semicoma brought on by lack of sleep. During the few hours of sleep I did get, I was beset by weird dreams. Now I was just alert enough to notice that no sudden cold snap had occurred overnight. Claudia's tape recorder would not be melting in a hot radiator.

I didn't see Marty's car parked in the driveway until the sudden blare of the horn pierced the still morning air — and, very nearly, my eardrums.

"Oh, Marty," I mumbled. "What a surprise." I staggered over to the car and nearly fell in. "Are you here to pick me up?"

"Yeah. Terry doesn't want me to drive her anymore." He sounded depressed.

"Stupid Terry. Just because you're not going together is no reason to give up a perfectly good chauffeur."

"She told you?" We backed out of the driveway.

"Yup." I let my head flop back against the seat.

"Did she say I was a perfectly good chauffeur?"

"No," I said, a little confused. "*I* said that."

"You said that to her?" Now he sounded confused.

"No, dummy, I just said that to *you*."

We stopped at the stop sign on the corner. He turned to look at me. "What's the matter with you today? You sound weird."

"I am suffering from terminal lack of sleep," I said darkly. "Wake me when we get to school." I closed my eyes.

Marty talked about Terry but I didn't hear a word he said. I had a plan for rescuing Claudia's tape recorder, but if I kept moving and thinking in slow motion like this, I would be useless. Perhaps I could catch a nap in Biology.

Unfortunately we had a surprise quiz in Biology so I didn't get to nap. On the other hand, the shocking realization that I could only take wild guesses at four out of the ten questions was a real eye-opener. I couldn't even guess at the other six — and surely "mitosis" did not mean "bad breath."

So when I met Peter outside the lunchroom after fourth period, I was quite awake.

"I only need three minutes in that office," I told him. "We'll call her from the pay phone again. If she falls for it don't let her spot you when she comes down the hall. After that number you did yesterday she's going to be suspicious if she sees us hanging around again."

Peter nodded. "I'll make the phone call."

"Oh no you won't! You just keep your eyes open and your back turned and tell me when she passes us."

"How can I keep my back turned and my eyes opened?" Peter demanded.

"Look, you stand outside the front entrance." I pointed to the main doors. "I can see you from the phone and you can see in. When she goes by, wave to me. My back will be to her, so she won't see me and she'll never notice you if you're not right in front of her in the hall. Got it?"

"Check," said Peter. "Good thinking." He sprinted out the door and plastered himself up against the glass, peering in. His nose was squashed against the pane. Several students clustered outside looked curiously at him. I shook my head impatiently and pantomimed a relaxed slouch. He caught on right away. He nodded and removed his nose from the glass. He put his hands behind his back and began to stroll in a little circle, whistling.

That was as casual as Peter was going to look. I sighed and dialed Mr. Fell's office.

"May I speak to Mr. Fell, please?"

"I'm sorry, he's out to lunch. May I help you?"

"Maybe you can. This is *mumpff* in the cafeteria. We have a little problem here. Do you think you could come down and help us straighten it out?"

"*Who* is this? What kind of a problem?"

"There seems to be some kind of a mix-up. If you could just come down here I'm sure you could straighten it out in a few minutes. It's very important and I'm sure Mr. Fell would want to know about it."

I hung up before she could respond. My heart was pounding and my palms were wet. Because for the first time since I planned the caper I was thinking of my father. "HEAD GUIDANCE COUNSELOR'S DAUGHTER BUSTED FOR BUGGING." That was the headline I should have considered. What in the world would they do to my father if I were caught? And why hadn't I thought of it when I dreamed up this crazy plot?

The bugging of Mr. Fell's office was insane, dangerous, and almost certainly illegal. I had never done anything like this before, and if I just managed to get the tape recorder out of Mr. Fell's heat vent safely, I vowed I would never do anything like it again.

Peter was waving wildly to me. I turned around and saw the back of Mrs. Chavez's red head bobbing down the hall.

She fell for it! I raised my eyes in silent thanks and promised that if I just got out of this alive I would be a good girl for the rest of my life. Peter was at my side in a flash and I had to force myself not to run down the hall to Mr. Fell's office.

"It worked, it worked," he crowed.

"Shut up, shut up," I panted.

He stood guard outside the office and I dashed straight into Mr. Fell's cubbyhole. Now I was glad that I hadn't had time the day before to put the screws back into the vent cover. All I had to do was lift it up and snatch the recorder out, which I did. I dropped it into my bag and replaced the vent. I didn't even bother with the screws now; if anyone ever noticed they were missing they'd never figure out why.

I darted out of the office, past the leather couch and the sunflowers on the wall. I grabbed Peter by the elbow and hissed, "Let's get out of here!"

"Boy, that was fast," he marveled. "You're good at this."

I put my hand against my heart as if I could control its wild hammering with a touch. "No," I whimpered as we beat a hasty retreat, "no, I'm really not."

There was no time to listen to the tape before I got to the *Log* office that afternoon so I had no idea what — if anything — was on it.

Only Chip, Bob, and Jessie Krause were in the office when I got there. I knew Peter would come as soon as he could, because he was burning to find out if we had gotten any evidence.

All three looked up curiously as I shut the door behind me.

Prudie Tuckerman was nowhere in sight.

I reached into my purse and pulled out the recorder.

"I have something for you," I said to Chip. "At least, I might have something for you."

"What is it?" he asked.

"It might be nothing. And then it might be — well, let's just listen."

I put the recorder on the front table and pushed the Rewind button. Nothing happened.

"Something's wrong with it," I muttered. "It was working yesterday."

"Maybe the batteries —" Bob began.

"That's right! It's been on for twenty-four hours!" Relieved, I hauled the cord out of my bag and stuck it in the machine. I looked around. "Where's an outlet?"

"Why has it been on twenty-four hours?" asked Jessie.

"It's a long story."

We found an outlet in the back of the room. I pushed the plug in and pressed the Rewind button. The whirring sound of the tape being set back to the beginning was reassuring.

I pressed the Play button. The first sounds I heard were recognizable only to me: a few mangled notes of Beethoven's Fifth Symphony, whistled off-key; the heat vent being put back on; the thud as I bumped my shin against Mr. Fell's desk.

"What in the world —" began Jessie.

As if on cue the Phantom Whistler stuck his head in the door and looked around.

"Am I late?" he asked in a loud stage whisper.

"No, we just started. Come on in," I said. Peter closed the door and tiptoed to the back of the room, where we stood huddled around the recorder.

For several minutes there was nothing on the tape but

a short, muffled conversation, which was Peter and me explaining to Mrs. Chavez that we had to leave. You couldn't make out the words but you could tell they were voices. Then, for a while, just some faraway clicking sounds which I realized must be Mrs. Chavez's typing.

"What is this?" asked Chip. "What are we supposed to be hearing?"

"I don't know," I said. "I told you it might be nothing."

"But if it *is* something," said Bob, "what exactly is it?"

"I don't want to tell you if it turns out to be nothing." It would be just as well that no one knew what I had done if I had no evidence.

I moved the tape up with the Fast Forward button.

Nothing. I kept moving it up and moving it up until there was very little tape left on the cassette.

"Whatever you think you got," Bob said dryly, "I don't think you got it."

I glanced at Chip. He stood with his arms folded, looking slightly bored and even a little irritated. I was wasting his precious time.

Then there was a new sound on the tape. "Shh!" I warned. A scrape, as if of moving furniture, then something that could have been drawers opening and shutting.

And then, nice and loud and perfectly recognizable, the sound of a telephone being dialed.

Peter clutched my arm so hard that his fingers nearly met at my bone. "This is it!" he cried. "This is it!"

"*Shh!*"

"Denton? Fell here."

Jessie shrieked. Chip's mouth dropped open. Bob slapped me on the back in glee. "You did it!" he bellowed. "You bugged his phone!"

"How did you do it, Carrie?" Chip stared at me, his face full of admiration. "How in the world did you do it?"

"*We* did it," Peter said proudly.

"Never mind how," I said. "Let me set the tape back so we can hear if we've got anything. You were all yelling so much —"

I pushed the Rewind button. "There."

"Denton? Fell here. My secretary told me you called. Yes? Oh, you think so? That much? Hogs, huh? You mean, instead of beef? Oh, yes, I see. Well, sure, if you think the profit outweighs the risk. Oh, sure, I know there's always a risk — name of the game, right? Ho ho. Yes, that's true, meat's meat. Hogs, beef, what's the difference? As long as we make out —"

There was a little hiss as the tape stopped.

"That's it," I sighed. "That's all I've got."

Chip's eyes glittered. He let out his breath with a deep *whoosh*, as if he'd been holding it for the full length of the tape.

He grabbed me around the shoulders and gave me a big hug.

"Carrie, this is fantastic! I knew that guy was a crook!"

"But what does it mean?" asked Peter.

"It's so simple," said Chip. "Don't you see?"

I leaned back against him, enjoying the feel of his arms around me once again. It had been a while. Now I was sorry Prudie wasn't here. I wanted her to see me like this with Chip, to realize that while she might have been a temporary distraction, over the long haul Chip would stick with me. But he dropped his arms and turned to Peter.

"It's the old substitution game. Just what I thought."

Jessie shook her head. "I don't get it either. It sounds sneaky, but what is he doing?"

"Look, if hogs are cheaper than beef and he says he's ordering beef, but orders hog meat instead —"

"*Oh!*" Bob and Peter got it at the same time.

"*Hog* meat?" cried Jessie. "We're eating *hog meat?*"

"Didn't you hear what he said? About profit and risk? And that thing about 'meat's meat, what's the difference as long as we make out'? Play it again, Carrie."

I rewound the tape and played it again.

"You're right," Jessie said indignantly when the tape had finished. "It's right there, plain as can be. What a racket. *Hog* meat. Yecch."

"How *did* you do it, Carrie?" Bob asked.

"*We* did it," Peter repeated. He pointed to me and then to himself. "Together. Both of us."

"Good work, Peter." Chip shook his hand.

Peter glowed.

"Let's go, Carrie," Chip said eagerly. He sat down at a typewriter and pulled a chair next to him. He gestured for me to sit down.

"We have to get the copy to the printer's in three days. Let's get this written up right now. I'll have to do a rewrite on the stuff I got from Cottage Cheese. We'll make it one big blockbuster and show how the graft starts right at the top and trickles down to the lowest level. Oh, this is fantastic!"

I sat down next to Chip and watched him pound away at the typewriter. Just briefly I wondered where Prudie was. But it really didn't matter. Things had, miraculously, worked out just as I'd imagined them.

"*By C. J. Wasserman and Chip Custer.*" That was the way it would be — in real life, as well as on the *Log*.

Eat your heart out, Prudie Pie.

╡[X]╞

You are invited to dinner
October 25 . . . 8 p.m.
Prudie Tuckerman
144 Cypress Hill Road
To celebrate the first issue
of the Lincoln Log.

The invitation was addressed to "Miss Carey Wasserman."

"Who eats dinner at eight o'clock?" I grumbled.

"Rich people do," said Jen. "And all smart dinner parties are at eight."

"Smart dinner parties my foot. She's up to something." I had no illusions about why I was invited to Prudie's party. She must have invited the entire staff of the *Log*. Leaving me out would have been too obvious — even for Prudie.

"I'll bet she's filthy rich," Jen added. "All the rich people live in that neighborhood."

"How do you know?"

"Because Tina Kelly lives there and she's rich."

Tina Kelly is a friend of Jen's. My mother always refers to Tina as "the one whose chauffeur takes her to the orthodontist."

Now I remembered where Cypress Hill Road was. Although I didn't know anyone who lived there, I'd driven through the area plenty of times. It was towering trees, winding roads, and signs that said, "Private Driveway." It was stone fences and houses that you could hardly see from the road. Jen was right. Prudie must be filthy rich.

Oh, swell.

Not only was she beautiful, but rolling in money. What a combination. Talk about your unfair advantages. I could picture Chip having a serious talk with Prudie's father in Mr. Tuckerman's leather-furnished, book-lined library.

"Mah daughtah tells me you want to work on a news-pay-pah, that raht, son? Which one would you lak? Ah own a few. You take cay-ah of mah little girl, and Ah'll

93

take cay-ah of you. Now, no moah of this 'Mistah Tuck-ahman' nonsense. You just call me 'Daddy,' heah?"

"What are you going to wear?" asked Jen.

"Oh my God, I have no idea. What do you wear to a dinner party?" If the hostess were anyone else but Prudie, I would call up and ask what she was wearing. But I didn't want Prudie to think I was the least bit insecure or that I thought her dinner was anything out of the ordinary. Even though I was a great deal insecure and had never been to a dinner party in my life.

"Elegant simplicity is in," Jen said.

"Elegant simplicity is always in, but I don't think I have a thing that fits the category." I went to my closet and started shoving hangers back and forth. I knew I didn't have anything suitable in there but I looked any-way, as if my fairy godmother might have paid a visit when my back was turned.

"There's plenty of simple stuff," Jen said, fingering a few short dresses, "but I don't see anything elegant."

"I don't *own* anything elegant."

"So you'll buy something."

"I don't even know what to buy! Mom! *Help!*"

Chip and Jessie had taken the final proofs of the *Log* to the printer's a week before the paper was due to come out. Mr. Thatcher had not even wanted to read the copy, which made me a little nervous. Mr. Gross had al-ways read over every story that we were going to print and it gave you a feeling of security to know that he was there as a backup, to make sure you didn't run a story that was going to get you in any trouble.

He never censored us. He'd never told us to "kill" an article, but then, we'd never done a story like "LUNCH PROGRAM RIDDLED WITH CORRUPTION!" before. Even though Chip was convinced we had the evidence, and even though he trusted Cottage Cheese completely, I would have been reassured if Mr. Thatcher had at least glanced at the story that was going to be run under my by-line.

Cindy and her circulation staff picked up the paper at the printer's on Friday, the day before Prudie's dinner. The boxes of newspapers would be stored in a locked closet in the *Log* office over the weekend, and Cindy would get them distributed first thing Monday morning. Chip planned to bring one copy to Prudie's party, let everyone see it, and then destroy it to prevent any advance leaks.

The security measures were only slightly less stringent than if the Premier of Russia were coming to address a Lincoln assembly.

Chip had been preoccupied with *Log* business for the whole week before he took the paper to the printer's, so that he had very little time to spend with Prudie. Not that she didn't try. She was "just dyin' to hey-ulp" so Chip attempted to teach her how to count type for headlines.

Anybody else could have taught her. Bob, in fact, eagerly volunteered, but since Chip and I had finished writing our lunchroom exposé, Chip said he had a little time to do it himself. Fortunately he didn't have too much time, and he soon gave up.

While Prudie seemed to understand how to count the letters ("*M* gets one and a half counts, so does *W*. All the rest get one, except *I* and lower-case *L*, which get a half"), she had trouble thinking up headlines to fit the spaces she had to work with. She kept coming up with these bizarre combinations like:

> LINCOLN ELEVEN
> CRUSHES BYRNES
> ELEVEN ELEVEN
> TO NOTHING ! ! !

and

> LE CERCLE FRANCAIS
> CELEBRATES CUISINE
> DE FRANCE WITH NEW
> ADVISERESS AT HELM

"Adviseress?" I asked, checking Prudie's headline.

"That was the only way Ah could make it fit."

"But with the *M* and the *W* and the *L*'s and the *I*'s it doesn't fit anyway."

"This is a — um — very confusing headline, Prudie," Bob said. "There are a couple too many 'elevens' in it. And we can use numerals for scores, you know. But it's really good," he added, "for your first try. Very — uh — imaginative. Eye-catching, even."

Anyhow, after Chip decided that headlines were not

Prudie's thing, he temporarily went back to being busy with dummying-up the paper, and Prudie went back to merely hanging over his shoulder and onto his every word.

But the week before her party . . . the week while the *Log* proofs were at the printer's, and there was no real *Log* business for Chip to do . . .

That week, which I spent mostly at every store in the Westfield Mall that sold clothes in size 7, I never saw Chip alone. I mean, not only did I never get a chance to see him when there was no one else around, but I never saw him without Prudie by his side.

I kept asking Jessie and Cindy what they were planning to wear on Saturday, and they kept telling me that they couldn't decide either.

I was driving myself crazy over a stupid dress for a dinner party, while the hostess was eyeing my boyfriend for dessert.

What could I do? A hundred plans ran through my mind, most of them ridiculous and all of them illegal. Killing Prudie would be the most effective, except that I couldn't be sure that Chip would wait thirty years till I got out of jail. I toyed with an anonymous note, but I didn't know what I should write, or to whom. "Keep your cotton-picking hands off Chip Custer or we will TAKE CARE OF YOU"? Or one to Chip that said, "PRUDIE TUCKERMAN HAS A VERY UNPLEAS-ANT AND VERY CONTAGIOUS DISEASE. BE-WARE. A FRIEND"? Perhaps if I could get a few strands of her hair, a fingernail clipping or two, a shred of her clothing, I could make a nice voodoo doll and stick pins in it. . . .

But the week passed and I did nothing except snap at my family and cry a lot. There was nothing to do. I could only hope that Chip would eventually come to his senses.

Chip did offer to drive me to Prudie's party, which was something, but he was driving Bob, Jessie, and Peter Kaplan too. It was hardly as if he were going to be my date for the party. It was more like I was a member of his car pool.

Saturday evening came and I got dressed with as much enthusiasm as I would for a funeral. I wanted to be dressed right, and I certainly wanted to look good, but on the other hand, what difference did it make? No matter how good I looked, Prudie would look better. No matter *how* I looked, Chip wouldn't be looking at *me*. It was useless.

The only thing that kept me going now was pride. I would not let Prudie see that she'd totally demoralized me. I would not let her think that I was giving up and planned to spend the rest of my life with stringy hair and shapeless clothes, feeding liver to the ninety-seven cats that lived with me as substitutes for human companionship.

I blew my hair dry, got into my reasonable facsimile of an elegantly simple dress, and applied makeup with extreme caution.

I stood back from my mirror and surveyed the results.

Not bad, I had to admit. The dress was midnight blue with long sleeves. It was short; Jen had been pushing for a long skirt, but I thought that might be a little too much. I tied my hair back with a narrow, blue velvet ribbon, and had borrowed an airy, cream-colored mohair shawl from my mother. I thought I looked about as elegant and sophisticated as I could look.

It might not make much of a difference, but at least I would know that I had gone out in a blaze of glory instead of a fizzle of frowsiness.

Jen came into my room just as I finished the survey. She had been dressing for the eighth-grade dance, which was also that night.

"Wow! Carrie, you look fantastic!"

"You don't look so bad yourself." She looked great. Although her dance wasn't to be dressy, she'd gotten a new skirt and a soft, fuzzy sweater and had, I guess with my mother's help, piled her hair on top of her head with two enameled combs.

"Carrie," she said hesitantly, "would you do me a favor? When Craig comes, would you stay up here?" She glanced at herself in my mirror. "Next to you I look positively *drab*."

"Oh Jen!" I hugged her. "You're positively wrong, but that's the nicest thing anyone's said to me all week."

I was starving by the time Chip honked his horn at 7:45. I couldn't believe rich people waited until eight for dinner. How did they survive the hours between lunch and now?

I remembered the scene in *Gone with the Wind* where

the girls all eat before going to this big barbecue, so that at the barbecue they'll only pick at tiny portions of food in order to give the impression that they're feminine and delicate and eat like little birds. That's what I should have done, I realized, as Chip honked again.

I should have had dinner before going to the dinner. Right now I felt I could eat a horse, and would probably eat *like* one, stuffing food into my mouth with both hands at once. While Prudie, who has no doubt seen *Gone with the Wind* forty-seven times and whose home life is probably similar to Scarlett O'Hara's, will hardly lift fork or knife at all — leaving her hands free to wrap Chip around her little finger.

I ran downstairs adjusting the mohair shawl.

"You look gorgeous," my mother said. "Have a good time."

"Carrie, stop a minute so I can see you," my father said.

I stopped. I turned at the bottom of the stairs, letting the full impact of my elegant simplicity hit him.

He nodded. "You should go to dinner parties more often," he said. "You look downright *regal*."

"Oh, thank you!" I ran to hug him. Now I *felt* downright regal. Instead of rushing I walked slowly, elegantly to the door, descended the front steps, and glided — regally, regally — to the driveway. I felt like I should have had a chauffeured limousine. Unfortunately, I had a ten-year-old Volkswagen already overstuffed with passengers.

"Climb in, Carrie," Chip said. At least someone had been thoughtful enough to leave the front seat, next to Chip, for me. Someone, I guess, still thought Chip was my boyfriend.

Jessie was stretched across the laps of both Peter and Bob in the back seat. She looked extremely uncomfortable.

"You look beautiful, Carrie," she said.

I ducked into the car. "Thank you. Isn't that a little . . . cramped back there?" Jessie is five foot ten.

"It's easier this way than to sit normally," she said. "My legs are too long. Otherwise Bob could sit on *my* lap."

"My legs are too long too," said Peter. "But if I put them over the front seat Jessie will have no place to sit."

"And you'll kick me in the head," Chip commented.

I closed the door and turned to face him.

"Hi there," I said softly.

For a moment, Chip didn't say anything. He just looked at me.

"You look . . . different," he finally said.

"My hair, I guess. It's pulled back."

"*Nice,*" he breathed.

My heart jumped violently, just once. He noticed! He isn't so blinded by Prudie's dazzling beauty that he doesn't see me! He still likes me. Maybe he even told the others to sit in the back; maybe it was *his* idea to save the front seat for me.

He backed out of the driveway and shifted gears. I

touched his hand lightly, without even thinking, as he shifted. There was a sudden, grinding noise.

"Don't do that when I'm driving, Carrie," he said gruffly.

From the back, I heard Peter giggle.

{XI}

Although it was just about dark by the time we got there, you could see that Prudie's house qualified as your basic mansion. Well, maybe not exactly a mansion, but the closest thing to one that I had ever seen. We turned in at a sign that read PRIVATE DRIVE. TUCKERMAN and followed the road for about half a mile before we saw the house.

"Holy cow," said Bob.

"It's huge," Jessie said. "You could fit six of my house in there."

"Maybe it's a two-family," Peter suggested.

The house had three floors and windows the size of my

front door. The entryway was lit by an overhead lantern and had enormous, dark wood double doors with brass handles.

Chip parked the Volks in a large, graveled area in front of the garages, which were approximately the size of a stable. There were three other cars there already, one of which Chip recognized as Cindy's ancient Skylark.

"Why do I feel," asked Jessie as she struggled out of the car, "like I ought to be arriving in a Rolls-Royce?"

"I can't imagine," I said.

Jessie was wearing a long skirt and a white blouse and carried a heavy sweater over one arm.

"You look really nice," I said, "now that I can see you."

"Thanks. I hope I'm not all wrinkled."

We walked to the front entrance, all huddled together as if for protection. I wished Chip would hold my hand, but he didn't. I almost put my hand on his arm, just for reassurance, but I was afraid he might say, "Don't do that while I'm walking, Carrie."

I felt very alone, even in our little group. How different this evening would be if Chip still cared about me. I wouldn't feel nervous, insecure, out of place, lonely. I'd be looking forward to a new, exciting experience, an opportunity to live, for a few hours, the sort of life I'd only seen in movies.

But Chip didn't care about me anymore. No matter what I'd thought at first when I got into the car, I was sure now that there was no hope. I might not know much about love, but I was bright enough to realize that if you love someone you don't snap at them for wanting to touch you.

I think we were probably all surprised when Prudie herself opened the double doors to let us in. I'm sure I wasn't the only one who expected a butler to greet us.

"Hah they-ah! Ah'm so glad you could come."

Now I don't know what I imagined Prudie would wear. I suppose something soft and fluffy, with a hoop skirt and flounces that would billow out from her sixteen-inch waist, and which would fit everyone's stereotype of Southern femininity. Just goes to show you.

In fact, Prudie was wearing a man-tailored, three-piece black velvet pantsuit over a white satin shirt. A little ruffle peeked through the sleeves of her jacket at her wrists and the front of the shirt was ruffled too. The shirt was gathered at the neck, with a very narrow black velvet ribbon that was sort of like a string going through it.

There was the essential difference between Prudie and me. If I had worn that outfit, I would have looked like a boy. Prudie could wear a man-tailored suit and look even more sexy than she would in a slinky dress with a neckline down to *here*.

I glanced at Chip, hoping that his face would reveal what was going on in his mind.

His mind was about as hard to read as a stop sign. His mouth hung slightly open, giving him a rather dim-witted air. He closed it only to gulp once or twice. When the folded-up copy of the *Log* he was holding fluttered out of his limp fingers to the floor, he didn't even notice.

He had all the symptoms of the shock victim; I was tempted to fling him to the floor, yell for blankets to cover him, and elevate his head until professional help arrived.

"Oh, the *Log!*" Prudie cried. She bent down and picked it up. "How excitin'! Come on into the library." (I knew it, I *knew* it.) "We'ah havin' cocktails in they-ah."

Cocktails! Jessie and I exchanged raised-eyebrow looks. Peter nearly clapped his hands in excitement.

Where were her parents? Did they know we would be drinking cocktails? Did they care? Of course, in a house this size, by the time the news reached them and they found their way to the library, a week might have passed.

Prudie told Jessie and me to leave our wraps on a bench and they would be put away safely in the cloakroom. (The *cloakroom!* A whole room just for cloaks? Or coats? My mother will die when I tell her. She claims that our overstuffed front closet is one day going to erupt in a hideous explosion, spewing boots, coats, sweaters, hats, umbrellas, and scarves all over the block.)

Chip, putting one foot carefully in front of the other like a drunk driver trying to walk a straight line, followed Prudie. The rest of us trailed after them across the huge front hall. The floor was black-and-white tile (marble?) and there was a long curving staircase on one side. Prudie's entrance hall was easily three times as large as our living room.

She opened a black-lacquered door and we followed her into the library.

Four of the kids from the *Log* were already there. The room was quite large and the little group in front of the fireplace was almost pathetic.

The library was exactly as I had pictured it, except for the fireplace, which I hadn't thought of, in which (of course; naturally) there was a roaring fire. Cindy greeted us with too much enthusiasm, so I figured she was feeling as awed and insecure as I was.

Along with Cindy were two members of her circulation staff, Larry Kollwicz and June Schneider. Paul Cruz, the art editor, stood with his back to the fire, looking entirely different in a blazer and slacks than he did in his school clothes, which seemed to consist of nothing but plaid flannel shirts and jeans.

Prudie went to answer the door again, though I hadn't heard a doorbell, and Chip's head swiveled around to watch her as she walked out of the library. I sighed and wandered over to the fireplace. I stood next to Paul, who was holding a glass of something.

"What are you drinking?" I asked.

"Vodka martini."

Vodka martini! How sophisticated that sounded. Prudie really was serving liquor to minors! She was a minor *herself*. Of course I knew some kids had beer at their parties — with or without their parents' knowledge — but vodka martinis! Wait till I tell my parents about this!

"Is it good?"

Paul shrugged. "It's booze," he said simply.

"Oh, it's got a little olive in it and everything, just like a real martini," I said, peering into the glass.

"It *is* a real martini," he retorted. "It's just made with vodka instead of gin."

I nodded. Prudie came back into the room with three more people: Judy Lutz, the news editor, Kevin Cooper, our photographer and Ann Marcus, the copy editor.

"Now that we'ah all heah, whah don't we get our drinks and toast the *Log?*" Prudie said.

Obviously Prudie had not invited the whole staff as I'd thought, because we had about five contributors who helped with typing and proofreading who weren't there. Once again, Chip followed Prudie obediently over to a corner of the library where, for the first time, I noticed a man in a white jacket standing behind a table full of bottles and glasses.

Those of us who didn't have drinks yet clustered in front of the table.

"Harold will make you anythin' you want," Prudie said.

So that's where the butler was. Serving the drinks. Of course.

"What should I have?" Peter asked excitedly. "Carrie, what are you going to have? I don't know what to ask for."

I finally got my first good look at Peter's dinner party clothes, not having paid much attention to him before. He was truly dazzling tonight in a mustard-gold suit with an open-necked purple-and-gold print shirt. His belt buckle was a copper replica of a Coors beer label.

"Paul is drinking a vodka martini," I said.

"Carrie, what'll you have?" Prudie asked sweetly. *She had her hand on Chip's upper arm.* Chip did *not* say, as he tilted his glass to his lips, "Don't do that while I'm drinking, Prudie."

Now I hadn't firmly decided that I was going to drink at all. I'm not a drinker, and I knew that being inexperienced with alcohol, I might very well get drunk on my first sip of anything and make an utter fool of myself. I had a glass of champagne with my parents on New Year's Eve, but I'd never really had an overwhelming urge to get plastered.

I was also sure that my parents would not want me to drink, but wouldn't throw me out of the house if they found out that I did.

I looked at Prudie's delicate white hand resting comfortably on Chip's gray blazer. Somehow I didn't feel like I wanted to be Miss Goody-Two-Shoes Wasserman right now. Somehow, I couldn't picture myself saying, under these circumstances, "I'll just have ginger ale, thank you," in a prissy little voice.

Drastic situations call for drastic measures. But what would my parents say if I came home loaded?

The hell with that.

"I'll have a — um —"

"Whah don't you try a Brandy Alexander," Prudie suggested. "Girls usually lahk that and Harold makes a delicious Brandy Alexander, don't you, Harold?" The perfect little hostess.

"Sure," I said recklessly. "I'll have one."

"What do boys like?" whispered Peter.

Prudie giggled adorably. "We have everythin'," she

said. "Maybe you'd lahk an Old-fashioned. That has a lot of fruit and stuff in it."

Peter nodded. "I like fruit."

Jessie and Judy and I got Brandy Alexanders, which did not look like any drink that anyone else was having. It looked all creamy, like a milkshake or something.

Peter choked and held onto his glass for dear life. He staggered away from the group.

"What's the matter?" Cindy asked him.

"Except for the fruit," he gasped, "I think this is straight liquor."

I sipped my Brandy Alexander cautiously.

It was incredible. It was absolutely delicious. Why, there could hardly be any booze in here at all. It tasted too good. Sweet, frothy; it had thick shakes beat all hollow.

After a few sips I looked around for Chip. He had his glass in one hand and the copy of the *Log* in the other. *He and Prudie* were going from person to person, showing everyone the *Log*.

I wondered what he was drinking.

Peter coughed in my ear.

"I could get bombed," he said, "just eating the fruit in this thing."

"You should have had one of these." I held up my half-empty glass. "It's delicious. You don't even taste the liquor."

"That's a girl's drink," Peter said. "Prudie said girls like it."

"You'd rather drink something masculine that makes you choke?"

"Of course," said Peter.

Prudie and Chip got around to us. I took only a brief look at the huge banner headline on the *Log*. I was more interested in my personal problems than in my career as a crusading reporter right now. I had forgotten that I was supposed to forget about men.

"It really looks great, Chip," I said hastily, getting that out of the way. "What are you drinking?"

His eyes looked sort of glazed and he hesitated a moment, as if he had to think about it. He looked blankly at his glass, trying to remember what was in it. Prudie's hand rested lightly on *his back* now. He was either drunk or simply intoxicated by the nearness of her.

"Oh. Yeah. Ginger ale."

Ginger ale? Oh, what a fine person he was! What a moral, upright, self-confident boy! Everyone around him was swilling liquor, acting, or trying to act, as if they were accustomed to nipping on a regular basis. But peer pressure had no effect on Chip. He didn't feel like drinking, so he didn't drink.

I wanted to cry. He was so good, so strong, so self-assured. But . . . if he looked drunk and wasn't drinking, that meant that he was in this dazed state because of Prudie Tuckerman.

I downed the rest of my Brandy Alexander.

Stupid, dumb Chip.

"We didn't toast the *Log* yet," Prudie said. "Oh, well.

111

We can do that at dinner, with the champagne. We'd better go in now. We have just a lovely dinner, and Ah wouldn't want everyone to be too . . . stinko to enjoy it."

I put my glass down on a table, probably an extremely valuable table that did not like damp glasses to be put down on it. *I* certainly wasn't stinko. It was a little warm in the library, but that was probably because of the roaring fire. I would be glad to get into the dining room, where it ought to be cooler. I tripped over Peter's foot — nothing serious, he caught me in time — and we all marched into the dining room.

"Who cares about food," Judy Lutz said dreamily. "Just give me another of those Alexander things."

"Keep walking, Judy," I said, watching her very closely as she moved ahead of me into the room, "or I will crash into you."

There was a long dining table in the dining room — which, I thought, is very logical, because where else would you expect a dining table to be? — with place cards. Cute little cards with our names on them, which were placed where Prudie wanted *us* placed. Prudie sat at the head of the table with Chip to her right and Paul on her left.

Clever Prudie.

I sat way down at the end of the table, between Bob and Peter. My place card read, "Carey Wassermann."

Mysteriously a man appeared and filled our wine glasses with champagne.

"To the *Log*," Prudie said, raising her glass.

"To the *Log!*" I cried. But nobody else said anything

so I felt a little self-conscious. Hastily I drank my champagne.

Strange, but it was still warm, even in the dining room. Well, that was probably because we were right next to the kitchen. You couldn't see the kitchen, of course, but you could assume that you were right next to it, as dining rooms are usually right next to kitchens.

I shook my head. This is a rich person's house, I told myself. There are servants. If you have servants to schlep things, you don't need to have your kitchen right next to your dining room. You could have your kitchen anywhere you wanted.

We began with soup.

"I don't think this is going to cool me off," I told Peter.

"Soup isn't supposed to," he replied.

"What kind of soup is it?" I asked.

"Prudie said it was green turtle," said June, who was sitting across from me.

Green turtle? As in *turtle*?

"I am not," I declared, "fond of green turtle soup."

I put down my spoon. It was, I noticed, one of six pieces of silverware at my place setting. I peered around Bob for a glimpse of Chip.

Chip was spooning his soup with precision regularity to his mouth, barely pausing to swallow. Chip is not normally a huge eater. Between her own delicate sips Prudie watched him with loving affection, like a mother enjoying her child's hearty appetite.

"How nice," I said. "Chip is fond of green turtle soup."

Bob patted my hand gently. "Carrie, drink some nice water."

"Thank you. I believe I will." I reached for the crystal goblet and drank some water. I drank all the water in the goblet.

That strange man appeared and filled my goblet from a pitcher.

I nearly jumped. "You surprised me," I said reproachfully.

"I'm sorry, miss."

"That's okay."

I saw a little plate of something in front of me that looked like a slice of pale meat loaf. I hadn't noticed it before.

"What is this?"

"That's pâté," said June. "It's good with champagne."

"Oh, like pâté de foie gras? I always wanted to try that. We learned about that in French. It has something to do with geese. The best stuff comes from Strasbourg. That's in France."

Bob gave me the oddest look. "Eat your nice pâté, Carrie. And *keep your voice down*," he hissed.

I scowled at him. "I am not shouting," I replied with dignity. "I am merely pleased to have this opportunity to sample pâté de foie gras."

I took a mouthful. "It's chopped liver!"

"*Shhh!*" Bob hit me in the shoulder.

I turned to him in outrage. "This is a classy dinner," I reminded him. "If you cannot act any better than a three-year-old you should not be here. People do not hit other people at classy dinners. That is extremely infantile."

"Carrie, *you are drunk*," he said between his teeth. "Eat that pâté, and those little pickles, and shut up until you get some more food in you."

Drunk? How could I be drunk? There was hardly any liquor at all in my Brandy Napoleon, and I've had champagne before, so how could I be drunk? Of course, I hadn't eaten anything since lunch, so I was probably a little weak from hunger, but I certainly wasn't *drunk*.

"I am merely," I whispered, "disappointed that all these years I've thought pâté de foie gras was something special and it turns out to be plain old dumb chopped liver."

"*Carrie!*"

"That's all right though. I am very fond of chopped liver."

Someone replaced our soup plates with little dishes of some pink stuff with a red sauce.

I eyed it suspiciously. "I believe that this is imitation shrimp cocktail."

"No, Carrie," June said. "It's Crab Louis."

"How do you know all these things?" I asked with admiration. "Do you frequently attend classy dinners?"

June smiled. "No. Prudie's been telling us what each course is when it comes out. You haven't been listening."

"Oh." I peered around Bob again to look at Prudie. She was talking to Chip. Chip was enjoying his Crab Louis.

Well, if Chip was enjoying his Crab Louis, so would I.

Two can play at that game. I chuckled softly.

Actually, the Crab Louis was awfully good.

I turned to Peter and found that he was staring at me, his eyes slightly glazed.

"This is delicious, isn't it?" I said, holding up a forkful of crab and sauce.

Peter didn't answer.

"Have I told you," I went on, "that you look positively resplendid this evening?" That didn't sound right. "I mean, splendent." That didn't sound right either.

He grabbed my left wrist, which fortunately was not holding my fork, but resting in my lap. (Even I know enough not to put my elbows on the table at a classy dinner party.)

"Carrie," he whispered urgently, "I love you."

For some reason that did not seem too surprising.

I put down my fork. I put my hand over his and said, with great compassion, "I know. But we must never speak of this again." I patted his hand and went back to my Crab Louis. It was really delicious.

Next came Beef Wellington. I listened carefully and this time I heard Prudie announce it. She sounded awfully far away. Well, it was a big table and I was all the way down at the end.

I'm afraid I began to giggle uncontrollably.

"Carrie, get hold of yourself." Bob stuck a Parker House roll in my hand. "Eat the nice roll."

"I can't help it. I just thought of a good joke."

"If you talk very quietly," Bob said, "you can tell me the joke."

"Okay. June!" I called across the table. "June, this is a

good joke. Listen. You too, Peter." Peter nodded. June stopped talking with Larry and turned to face me. I think Bob groaned.

"We had Brandy Napoleons, right?"

"Alexanders," Peter corrected.

"Right, Alexanders. Then we had Crab Louis, right. Then Beef Wellington. The whole dinner is named after war heroes, so for dessert we should have Pershing melon. Get it? Pershing melon?"

I cracked myself up. June laughed.

"I don't get it," said Peter.

"Me neither," muttered Bob. "And Louis was a king, not a war hero."

"Pershing melon instead of Persian melon," June explained. She was still smiling. June is a very intelligent person.

"I never heard of Persian melon," said Peter. "I never heard of *Pershing*."

"He was a famous general," I explained. "And Persian is a famous melon."

"Carrie," said Bob, "eat your nice dinner."

Well, it wasn't all that nice from the Beef Wellington on. Beef Wellington is a lot like roast beef except it has this pastry crust around each piece, which is cute, but rather flimsy. There were also potatoes and some vegetables in a gloppy sauce. After the Crab Louis, the dinner really went downhill.

Every once in a while I would turn to Peter and find him gazing at me mournfully, like a baby basset hound.

For dessert we had crème caramel.

"Oh, no Pershing melon?" I giggled. The man came to fill my water glass again.

"Oh, hello there. Is there any more champagne?"

"Carrie!"

"I'll see," he said.

He went to the head of the table and conferred with Prudie.

"He doesn't mind," I told Bob. "That's what he's here for."

The man came back and told me that champagne was no longer being served.

"Oh well. *C'est la vie.*"

I dug into my crème caramel. "This is custard," I announced, "with delusions of grandeur."

"Carrie," Bob said gravely, "will you promise me something?"

"That all depends." Crafty Carrie! No one was going to put anything over on *me*.

"Promise me you'll never take another drink until you're a big girl."

"Well!" Haughtily I turned my back on him.

"Carrie, you are bombed out of your mind," he whispered.

I turned back to face him. For some reason he looked very fuzzy. His nose was melting. I shook my head and blinked my eyes a few times. *He* must be the one that's drunk, I thought. *My* nose isn't melting. *I* don't look fuzzy.

On the other hand, I didn't have a mirror nearby — so maybe I looked fuzzy too. Maybe my nose *was* melting. I suddenly realized that I *felt* kind of fuzzy. At least, my head felt fuzzy. My face muscles felt very tight, like my skin was starched.

Was I really bombed out of my mind?

"If indeed I am," I said carefully, "it is *her* fault. *She* served alcohol to minors. She is guilty of imploring the manners of a moral." I frowned. I knew what I meant, but I don't think that was it. Oh, and I'd tried to say it so carefully, too!

"I think you mean," Bob hissed, "impairing the morals of a minor."

"Isn't that what I said?"

"Not quite. And you didn't have to drink if you knew you couldn't hold it."

Suddenly I felt very sad. "Why are you picking on me?" I whimpered. "How did I know I couldn't hold it? I never held any before."

I nudged Peter. "He is being very mean to me," I said. I pointed at Bob. Peter was hunched over his dessert plate. He didn't look at me. "If you truly loved me," I said, "you would punch him out."

Black coffee in tiny cups was served, along with cookies and little iced cakes. They were very cute. I do not drink coffee. I ate six little cakes.

"I am extremely thirsty," I said. "I wonder why that man doesn't come back and fill up my water glass."

"Drink mine," said Bob. He pushed his goblet toward me.

"That is extremely unsanitary," I replied. "You might have trench mouth, for all I know."

"Carrie, for heaven's sake!"

"Oh, all right. Thank you. I'm too thirsty to worry about trench mouth." I drank all his water.

Eventually it was time to go home. The party was over. For some reason Bob felt it was necessary to steer both Peter and me to the front hall. Although things looked a little blurred, I was quite capable of walking without assistance; I don't know about Peter.

Prudie was saying good-bye to everyone. She put her hand on Chip's arm again. Chip looked down at her, his face very serious and sober.

Ha ha, I thought. Your little plot didn't work, Prudie Python. He didn't drink, therefore you could not get him drunk and take advantage of him. I cackled softly.

It was all for nothing, this elaborately staged plot.

He took her hand and *squeezed it.*

I was going to cry. I leaned against Bob and moaned quietly.

His arm around my shoulder, he guided me out the door, grabbing my mother's shawl from Prudie and saying something — I don't know what — to our hostess.

The cold night air felt heavenly on my cheeks. What a relief to get out of that overheated barn.

We trudged to Chip's car.

"You sit in front, Jessie," Bob said. "I'll take care of the alkies in the back."

"What alkies?" Chip said vaguely.

"Little Carrie and little Peter. You were probably too busy to notice, but they're both smashed."

"I am *not* smashed," Peter said. "I'm just a little depressed."

Chip opened the car door and pushed the front seat down. Peter climbed in, then Bob.

Chip looked at me curiously. "Are you drunk, Carrie?"

"I am extremely morose," I said, with quiet dignity. I climbed into the back of the Volkswagen and fell onto Bob's lap.

"Oooff!" he grunted. "Carrie, take it easy."

"If I'm too heavy for you, just stick me in the trunk," I said, feeling very sorry for myself. "No one will care."

"You're not too heavy, you just sat down too hard. Stretch your legs across Peter. Peter doesn't mind, do you, Peter?"

"Peter doesn't mind *anything*," Peter said. "Do what you want to Peter. Treat him like dirt. It doesn't matter."

"Oh, God," Bob muttered.

Jessie twisted around in the front seat to look at us. She shook her head.

"I never realized this car was so bumpy," I complained as we chugged down Cypress Hill Road. "I would appreciate it if you would not hold your arms tightly across my stomach," I told Bob. "Anything tight around my stomach right now might be hazardous to my health."

"Oh, great," Jessie said. "Carrie, don't you dare get sick."

"I don't know where else I can put my hands," Bob said. "It's a little cramped back here, Carrie."

"You may put them on my elbows."

Chip drove Peter home first. Peter got out of the car. He seemed to be able to walk on his own. He'd almost reached his front door when he made a sudden, sharp veer to the right and leaned over some shrubbery.

"What's he doing?" asked Jessie.

"Throwing up in the bushes," Bob said.

Peter stumbled up his front steps and we drove away. Bob groaned as I slid off his lap and sat where Peter had been sitting.

"You're glad to get rid of me," I said sulkily.

He didn't deny it.

Jessie lived only a few blocks from Peter, so Chip dropped her off next. It would have made sense for him to take me home before Bob, because it was out of the way to do it the other way around, but Chip drove the long route to Bob's house.

Just as if we were still going together, I thought sadly.

Bob climbed out of the car. "Are you going to be all right?" he asked me.

"I don't know. At this point it's touch and go."

"Come in the front," Chip said.

"Why?"

"So you can sit next to me."

"Why would I want to sit next to you? I am perfectly fine back here. Morose, but perfectly fine."

"So I can keep an eye on you," Chip said.

"There's no need for that. I do not think I'm in any danger in the back seat of a Volkswagen. Alone."

"Come on, Carrie," said Bob. "I'll help you." He leaned in and took my hand. With great difficulty I climbed out of the back and slid into the front seat next to Chip. Bob closed the door. He looked across me to Chip.

"Good luck with her father."

"What do you mean?" asked Chip. "It's not my fault she's drunk."

Bob seemed very annoyed, though I couldn't figure out why.

"Don't be stupid, Chip."

We drove off. I leaned my head against the window frame, so the cool air could blow across my face. I sighed a few times. It was all so sad. Before I realized what was happening, two tears trickled down my cheeks.

Chip didn't say anything for a while. Finally, when we were stopped for a red light, he turned to me. "Carrie?" His voice was soft.

"What?"

"I — I — oh, Carrie, I don't know how to say it."

Suddenly there were a lot more than two tears. Whatever it was Chip didn't know how to say, I had a feeling I didn't want to hear it.

"You don't have to say anything," I sniffled. "Just drive me home and leave me on the front steps with a note pinned to my shawl."

My heart was breaking. I couldn't stop the tears. That was all I needed — eye makeup running all over my cheeks. How appealing I must look: a drunk, morose person with black-and-blue streaks down her face. I had no tissues and I certainly couldn't wipe my eyes on my mother's mohair shawl.

"Carrie, Carrie, I'm sorry." His voice was pained, almost desperate. Did he expect *me* to feel sorry for *him?*

"Did you really get drunk because I — I mean, I guess I didn't pay much attention to you at the party —"

"You didn't pay much attention to me all week," I said. "But I didn't get drunk because of that. I got drunk because I don't know how to drink."

"That's a load off my mind," said Chip. He sounded relieved. *Too* relieved. Why should he feel better when I was feeling so rotten?

"It's not your fault I got drunk," I went on. "But it was your fault I was *drinking.*"

"Oh, Carrie."

We pulled up in front of my house. Chip switched off the motor and turned toward me. "Carrie, I'm sorry, I really am. I didn't mean to hurt you."

"Does that mean" — I swallowed hard — "that you don't plan to hurt me anymore?"

"Carrie, I — oh, damn it, I just don't know what to say to you."

"Never mind. You answered the question. I suppose you can't help it if you don't like me anymore."

"Carrie, I still *like* you." He put much too much emphasis on the word "like."

It was over. I knew that now.

I had to get out of there. My heart was breaking, my stomach was churning, my mascara was running and I looked — and felt — disgusting.

I pushed the car door open and stumbled out. Chip ran out of the car and around to my side. "You can't go inside looking like that!" His voice shook. He was probably terrified of what my father would think. He gave me his handkerchief and I blotted my cheeks. I realized that I must look as bad as I thought I looked, which made me feel even worse.

He helped me up the front steps. I was kind of hunched over and every step seemed to trip me.

I hoped my parents were asleep, but lights were blazing all over the house.

My father opened the door.

"My God!" he cried. "What's the matter with her? Carrie, Carrie, are you all right? What happened?"

"Nothing, really," Chip said, his voice trembling. "She — uh, well, she sort of —"

"What? She sort of what?"

"I'm sorry," I croaked, "but I'm afraid I'm . . . stinko."

I pushed my way past my father and staggered to the bathroom.

{XII}

"Oh, God," I moaned. "Oh, God." I turned over in my bed and saw Jen sitting on the floor, staring at me.

"What are you doing here? Why are you watching me sleep?"

Sunlight was streaming through my windows. It was morning.

"I'm not watching you sleep. I'm watching you wake up. Do you know you're the first person I ever saw drunk? I mean, not like at weddings, but really *disgusting* drunk."

"Oh, God."

"So I wanted to see if you had a hangover. I've never seen a hangover before either."

"You were home last night when I got in?" I shielded my eyes from the sun.

"Oh, boy, was I! They talked about you for an hour after Mom and I put you to bed."

"You put me to bed?" I couldn't even remember it. "That's humiliating."

"You want to know what they said about you?"

"No. I have a feeling I'll find out. If I ever get up. Which I may not." I turned over and buried my face in my pillow. "I was awful," I mumbled. "Up until the time I got home, I remember *everything*. Every hideous thing I said. I thought drinking was supposed to make you forget."

"I can't understand a word you're saying. Don't talk into your pillow like that. How do you feel? Do you have a hangover?"

"How should I know? I never had a hangover before." I turned sideways to face Jen. "Close the blinds."

She did. "How do you *feel?*"

"My mouth tastes awful. Like something built a nest on my tongue. Get me a glass of water, will you?"

Jen brought back the water. I leaned up a little on my elbow and drank the whole glassful.

"Do you have a headache? Upset stomach?"

"No."

"Then I guess you don't have a hangover." She sounded quite disappointed.

"I have," I said grimly. "But it's a hangover of the *soul*."

I put the glass on my night table and lay back.

127

"Did you have a nice time at the dance?" Polite Carrie.

"It was okay. Craig is kind of drippy. He was afraid to kiss me on the lips because he wears braces too and he said he might get a shock. So you know what he did? He bowed down and kissed my *hand*. Isn't that dumb?"

"You made out better than I did," I said under my breath.

"I'll tell Mom you're up."

"No, don't. Not yet. Just tippy-toe out of here and leave me alone for a while. What time is it?"

"Nine-thirty."

Jen left my room, closing the door very quietly behind her. I stared up at the ceiling. There was a simple solution. I just wouldn't get out of bed. *Ever.*

Morbidly I played the whole evening back in my mind. It seemed that I could remember vividly every single stupid thing I'd said and done. I must have been revolting. Chip . . . oh Lord, what Chip must have thought of me.

It doesn't matter, I told myself. He was already out of love with me before I got drunk — after all, wasn't that the reason I'd let myself get drunk in the first place? So that no matter how repulsive I'd been, it wouldn't have made any difference.

But how would I face anyone tomorrow? Not just Chip, who had broken my heart, but Bob and June and Jessie and Peter — who had declared that he loved me. Well, maybe Peter wouldn't remember he said that. He'd been as blotto as I was, so he'd have his own regrets.

No, I simply wouldn't get out of bed. That was the

only answer. There was nothing to get out of bed *for*. I had finally and definitely lost Chip and made a fool of myself in front of the entire *Log* staff — except for five typists. What was left for me?

There was a gentle knock on my door.

"Please go away," I said weakly.

My mother opened the door and came into my room. "How are you feeling?"

"I'll live. More's the pity."

"We weren't so sure of that last night."

"Please," I begged, "don't lecture me. I can't stand it. I'll never do it again, I'll be a good girl as long as I live, lips that touch liquor will never be mine and all that crap."

My father peered through the doorway.

"You okay?"

"Dandy," I said hoarsely. "I'm sorry. I know you're disappointed and ashamed of me. But please, no lectures now."

"What lecture?" my mother said. "You just gave yourself the whole lecture without my saying a word."

"We're not ashamed of you," my father said.

"And after spending half an hour with you in the bathroom last night," added my mother, "while you begged us to put you out of your misery, I'm pretty convinced you'll never do it again."

"Did I say that?" I didn't remember the bathroom bit, or anything else that happened after I got into the house.

"You said if you were a horse and had a broken leg we would shoot you."

"I said a lot of clever things last night. How come you're not ashamed of me?"

My father shrugged. *"You're* the one who got drunk."

Dr. Wasserman the psychologist. I wasn't up to reasonableness any more than lectures.

"Okay. Good. Fine. I'm ashamed. Please leave me alone now."

"You want breakfast?"

"No. Maybe later."

I was still in bed at eleven-thirty when Claudia came over.

She came into my room without knocking and perched on the edge of my bed.

"So, how was the fancy dinner party? Did you just wake up?"

"No. I've been up for a while. I'm just not getting out of bed. Ever."

"What happened?"

"Oh, Claude, it was the worst night of my life. A three-star evening. I watched Chip slobbering over Prudie for three hours, I got drunk and made a fool of myself, and then I sniveled like a baby when Chip said he was sorry he didn't love me anymore."

"He said that?"

"Just about." I told her the whole, horrible story, from beginning to end. She shook her head every once in a while, and made little clucking sounds with her tongue. Claudia is a very sympathetic listener.

"You know what I think?" she said. "I think Prudie is like a virus. You don't get any medicine for a virus, you

130

just have it for a few days and it goes away by itself. All you can do is wait it out. It might be bad while you've got it, but it's temporary."

"Chip has it bad, that's for sure."

"Or like cotton candy," she said thoughtfully. "You know, sweet, delicious, but fluffy and not really substantial. That's what Prudie is. Cotton candy."

"I liked virus better," I said.

"Okay then. Virus."

"You really think so? You really think he'll get over her?"

"Yeah, I do. The only thing is we don't know how long it'll take. Or even whether you'll want him back when he's cured."

"Oh, Claude, I'll want him back, believe me. But what do I do in the meantime?"

She shrugged. "What you always do. Work on the *Log*, read good books, cry yourself to sleep."

I laughed bitterly. "I can do the last two without any trouble. But I swear, I don't know how I can face anyone tomorrow. I mean it. Claude, if you had been there you would have pretended you didn't know me. That's how embarrassing I was."

"As I see it," she said, "you have three choices. You can act as if nothing happened, and not mention it. Or you can laugh and make jokes about it. Or you can exaggerate how awful you were, which will make people feel sorry for you."

"I don't want people to feel sorry for me. And I *was* awful — I don't have to exaggerate that."

"Now listen. If someone says to you, 'Carrie, I'm such a terrible person,' what's the first thing you'd say?"

I didn't even have to think about it. "I'd say, 'No, you're not.'"

"Right. That's the natural response. You argue with a person who puts himself down, right? So if you go in tomorrow and someone brings up the party, and you say, 'I feel like such a fool, everyone must think I'm an idiot,' the natural response would be, 'Nobody thinks you're an idiot.'"

I pondered that for a minute. "But even if they say that, inside they'll be thinking I'm an idiot."

"No they won't," Claudia insisted. "They'll see you feel miserable and they'll *feel* for you. Not feel sorry for you," she added hastily, "just feel for you. And if anyone bugs you, or says something like, 'Boy, were you crocked,' just agree with them." She made a sad face. "You say, 'I know, and I feel just terrible about it.' That'll stop them in their tracks. I mean, what can they say after that?"

I thought it over. "Nothing," I said slowly. "You're right. That's really clever, Claude. I don't how you figure things out like that."

"It seems to come naturally," Claudia said.

I was beginning to feel a little better. Only an insensitive clod could keep hassling me after I admitted that I felt rotten about how I acted at Prudie's, and the *Log* staff in general was not made up of insensitive clods. And after all, only Bob, Jessie, June, Peter, and Chip had really seen me at my worst. Bob and Jessie certainly wouldn't be nasty about it, I knew that. Peter couldn't

132

be, since he'd be as worried about how he acted as I was about myself. June was a senior, and not the type to pick on pickled sophomores.

And Chip? Chip didn't care.

I felt a strange hollowness where my heart should have been. I realized that in a moment I was going to start crying again.

"Claude, you're right and you've been a big help and I *will* get up in a while, but would you go now, please? I can't — " My voice broke.

"Sure. I'll see you tomorrow." She patted my shoulder. "I know," she said softly. "Go on and cry."

She left, closing the door behind her.

I turned my face into the pillow and began to sob so hard that the bed shook beneath me. No matter how tightly I squeezed my eyes shut, I couldn't turn off the picture which the camera in my mind had snapped: Chip and Prudie, in his car, arms wrapped around each other, kissing passionately.

I cried until I had no tears left.

{XIII}

LUNCH PROGRAM RIDDLED WITH
CORRUPTION! GRAFT, MISREPRE-
SENTATION, FRAUD, SET PATTERN
FOR LIST OF LINCOLN SCANDALS!!

*Dairy Company Bribes Are Small Potatoes;
Deceit Starts Right at the Top!*

by Chip Custer and C. J. Wasserman

The Log has learned that the school lunch program at
Lincoln is rife with payoffs and rip-offs and that the
district director of the program himself is implicated in
the scandal.

The Log has hard evidence that the director of the program made a practice of substituting hog meat for beef,
thereby misrepresenting the meat served to students, and

lining his own pockets with the money he saved by purchasing cheaper meat.

According to a reliable source, the entire program is rotten with profiteering, bribery and graft, and although it starts with the "Big Fish" some of the "small fry" at the custodial and cafeteria level are also skimming some cream off the top.

Included among the rip-offs reported to the Log are:

*Bribes from the dairy company which supplies the district with milk, to cafeteria employees.

*The stealing of food and supplies from the cafeteria by employees, for their own personal use.

*Recycling of cooked food instead of disposal, thus leaving more fresh food available for the staff to take home.

Obviously an investigation is called for, and while the Log feels that the school district should be vitally interested in getting such an investigation under way immediately, we are willing to present our evidence to the district attorney if our own school board and the superintendent of schools are reluctant to rock the boat.

There was another, more detailed article next to this, outlining each charge in detail, with the information Chip had gotten from Cottage Cheese.

Marty had driven me to school that morning and I warned him that he was sworn to secrecy about ever having spoken to me regarding tape recorders. Two weeks ago, when I'd given Claudia back her cassette recorder, I'd sworn her to secrecy too.

Chip was holding the tapes — the original, and a copy he made for "insurance" — because I refused to have them in my possession. Only five of us knew who had gotten the tape and we all agreed no one else must ever know. I didn't have to spell it out for them; they could imagine the headline "HEAD GUIDANCE COUNSELOR'S DAUGHTER BUSTED FOR BUGGING!" as easily as I could.

To say that the first issue of the *Log* created a sensation would be like saying that the exploding of an atom bomb creates a small disturbance. "Sensation" is an understatement.

The school was in an uproar. Cindy and her circulation staff had gotten in early Monday and distributed copies of the paper to the homerooms. By first period, every student in the school must have read the article, because no one was talking about anything else.

I hadn't seen Chip yet, but I thought that he must be very pleased. I was glad for him. I didn't even worry about how I would face the people who had been at Prudie's when we had our staff meeting this afternoon. After the *Log*'s success they wouldn't even remember I had been drunk — they would just congratulate me on my part in the investigation.

Like all the people in my first two classes. I was swamped with praise, swarmed over by kids who wanted to shake my hand, slap me on the back, or find out how we'd gotten the goods on the cafeteria. It was so exciting, I almost forgot about Chip.

In Biology, Mr. Sachs stopped me as I came in the door.

"I didn't see my interview in the paper," he said, as if he hadn't even noticed the banner headlines across the front page.

136

Standing so close to his tall blondness, I felt my heart, which was still apparently in working order, go into that "flutter thump" bit. Well, why not? Go ahead and flutter, I told my heart. There's no reason in the world now why you cannot flutter for Mr. Sachs without feeling disloyal. Flutter all you want.

It did.

But I couldn't just stand there enjoying the nearness of Mr. Sachs. I had to think fast. He was waiting for me to explain why his interview was not in the *Log*. I didn't want to tell him he was too dull — or that the interview was.

"The editor thought that for our first issue we ought to have an article about our new adviser," I said. "We're going to do you in our next issue."

"Oh." He sounded kind of hurt.

"And I'd like to get some more information, if that's okay. I mean, we really want to do an in-depth article and I was kind of new at interviewing, like I told you, and didn't do a very good job the first time." Clever Carrie! Now I'd get to see him again and ask him more questions — and this time I'd have a nice, long list.

He brightened considerably. "Sure, that'll be fine." He seemed flattered.

I took my seat and accepted some more extravagant praise from my classmates. And that was the last pleasant moment I had for the rest of the day.

We were playing field hockey in gym when they sent for me.

I was standing in the goal, leaning lazily on my stick, entirely uninterested in whether or not anyone shot the ball past me. Being goalie is so *boring*. But running back and forth across the field is very tiring and I'm even lousier at chasing the ball and blocking out opponents than I am at standing in the net. Actually it's probably a toss-up, because I'm a really rotten goalie and the fact that the opposing team was ahead 6 to 2 was entirely my fault.

Anyway, someone brought out a note and gave it to Miss Dandridge, and Miss Dandridge yelled, "Time!" and called me over to her.

"You're wanted in the principal's office."

"*Me?* Now? Like this?" I looked down at my crummy, creased gym suit, which would make Raquel Welch look like a potato. "Can I change first?"

She shook her head. "The locker room isn't opened until the end of the period. You can't go in now. And they said immediately. So you'd better get on the stick."

Miss Dandridge is the only person I know who says, "Get on the stick."

I trudged across the field toward the school building. I couldn't imagine why the principal wanted to see me and I hated the thought of walking into school and down the hall in front of everyone, wearing this stupid, pale blue flour sack.

As I walked, I realized that of course it must have something to do with the *Log*. And I began to suspect that I was not being summoned to receive the Pulitzer Prize.

Why, I wondered, had I conveniently avoided thinking about the consequences of the story that ran under my name? Why hadn't I stopped to consider, for more than two minutes, the position in which I had placed my father? Why had I been so consumed with desire to be an investigative reporter that I had forgotten that investigative reporters frequently get *yelled at*? Why hadn't I read up on slander and libel laws?

By the time I got into school and down the hall to the principal's office, I was perspiring profusely, and it certainly wasn't because of my efforts on the hockey field. If anyone was snickering at my outfit, I didn't notice. One boy looked at my legs and made kissing noises, but I was trembling so hard that I was more concerned that my legs would support me than with how they looked.

Although I'd never been inside the principal's office, which was a room off the main office, there was a bench outside it, and many times I'd seen kids seated there, looking either sullen or terrified, waiting to be summoned into Mr. Bauer's presence.

This time when I went inside the main office, I found the entire staff of the *Log* lined up on the bench, with the overflow milling around the closed door marked PRINCI-PAL.

"Here's Carrie," Jessie said. "Now everyone's here."

"And doesn't she look stunning," teased Bob, "in her powder-blue bloomers. The latest thing in fashionable prison attire."

"Oh, shut up." They didn't seem very worried. But why should they? They hadn't put their names over the story that "ripped the lid off" the lunchroom.

Then why were they here? I felt very confused.

Peter Kaplan was sitting on the bench, head in his hands, mumbling. He looked worried. I was sure he was thinking about veterinary school.

Chip dragged himself away from Prudie's side and made his way over to me. His face was serious but calm. I wished, briefly, that I was not wearing my gym suit — but only briefly. How much more of a fool could I make of myself than I already had on Saturday night? Nothing I did, said, or wore now would lure Chip back.

"Carrie," Chip said in a low voice, "listen. I think there's going to be some trouble."

"I didn't think they called us here to congratulate us," I agreed.

"No." Chip's mouth twisted in a wry little smile. "I brought some insurance with me, just in case of something like this, but whatever you do, don't give them any information. You know what I mean?"

He looked at me hard. I knew he didn't want to say too much with all the other kids around; the kids who didn't know where the tape had come from, or even that there was a tape. I nodded.

"Don't volunteer anything," he went on. "Don't admit anything. A journalist can't be forced to reveal his sources."

"A student journalist can be kicked out of school," I pointed out.

"No, he can't," Chip said confidently. "Don't you worry about that. When they question you and ask why your name is on the story with mine, that's because you helped mc write it. Remember that — you just helped me with the writing."

He was protecting me! He didn't want me to get into trouble! Didn't that mean he must still care — at least a little?

I tried not to think about that now. It didn't seem the time or the place for worrying about romantic entangle-ments.

"But why is everyone else here? How come they didn't just call us down?"

"I don't know," Chip said. "But we'll find out in a minute." He raised his voice. "Okay, everybody, here we go."

He opened the door to the principal's office.

We all crowded in behind him, and crowded is the right word. Even though Mr. Bauer's office was consid-erably bigger than Mr. Fell's broom closet, it seemed strained to the bursting point with the entire staff of the *Log* crammed into it.

Mr. Bauer was seated behind a desk. Mark Thatcher, our adviser, was leaning against a window, apparently staring out at the flagpole. He didn't look at us when we came in. And then there was the third man.

He was enormous. He towered over everyone in the room, dwarfing even Peter. This man was at least six foot five, with shoulders as broad as a couch and a neck like a tree trunk. His hands were clenched into fists at his side, and the fists were the size of cantaloupes.

He did not look happy. His eyes were blazing. I had a

feeling that if he opened his mouth, spurts of flame would shoot out and incinerate us all on the spot.

"I want you to meet the man you libeled," Mr. Bauer said. "The man whose good name you dragged through the mud, the man you exposed to shame and ridicule and disgrace and criminal prosecution." His voice got louder and louder as he talked, until he was gripping the edges of his desk and practically screaming. "This," he shrieked, "is Nelson Fell."

Oh dear. I shrank back and tried, unsuccessfully, to hide behind Bob. Why couldn't Mr. Fell have been five foot two and skinny? I might not be in any less trouble than I was now, but at least I wouldn't have this sickening fear that he would break me in half like a toothpick at the first opportunity.

"Now, first of all, I want every copy of that scandal sheet confiscated."

There were groans of dismay and disbelief from the staff. Everyone began talking at once.

Mr. Bauer pounded on the desk. "That's why you're all here. Every single one of you is going to spend the rest of the day collecting those papers. I'll announce that the students are to hand in their copies when you come around to get them. I don't know how you'll do it, I don't care how you do it, but you'd better do it. How many copies are there?"

"Eleven hundred," Chip said evenly. "A hundred for the administration and teachers and a thousand for the students. But I don't know how you expect us to force the kids to give us back the papers. Once you announce that they *have* to give them up, they'll never turn them in."

"That," said Mr. Bauer, "is your problem. I'll be in the *Log* office at three this afternoon, and I expect to find one thousand copies of the paper there. I'll also expect to find all of you there. We have some talking to do about whether this school will continue to have a newspaper at all. You can go now. Except for Chip Custer and Caroline Wasserman. I'm not finished with you."

I gulped hard, as if I could swallow my fear. Someone patted me gently on the shoulder for reassurance. Prudie wiggled her fingers in a cheery good-bye wave at Chip. In moments the office was empty except for Chip and me and the three men.

The silence was terrifying. What was Mr. Bauer going to say, and why didn't he start saying it already? I looked down at my sneakers. "C. Wasserman" was printed across the toes. I stared at my name as if I had never seen it before.

"The first thing we'll discuss," said Mr. Bauer, "is how you'll word the retraction. And how you'll get it distributed."

"I don't see why," Chip replied calmly, "we should print a retraction for something that's true."

Nelson Fell roared. I thought he was about to spring at Chip's throat and I actually grabbed Chip's arm to pull him out of the way of the man's rage.

"You skinny punk!" he bellowed. His face turned purple. I began to shake with fear, and I wished I could hold my hands over my ears to shut out his screaming.

Chip waited until Mr. Fell ran out of curses and then said, still calm, "We have evidence of what we printed in that story."

"What evidence?" Mr. Fell snarled. "You're either lying or out of your mind."

I thought Chip was going to produce the tape, but instead he reached into his shirt pocket and pulled out a folded piece of paper. He unfolded it and handed it to Mr. Fell.

"This is a transcript of a conversation you had with a man named Denton," Chip said. "Do you recognize it?"

Mr. Fell read the paper. His lips moved as he read, as if he were re-creating the phone call in his mind. He frowned.

"Where did you get this?"

Chip shook his head. "I can't tell you that. We got it, that's all that matters."

"You think so?" Mr. Bauer asked menacingly. "You think eavesdropping and telephone tapping are legitimate sources of information?"

"Mr. Bauer, why don't you look at the transcript?" Chip suggested. "If Mr. Fell will show it to you. You were very concerned that Mr. Fell's good name was ruined by our story, but now that I tell you we have evidence that supports our story, you're threatening us because we *got* the evidence."

Suddenly there was a roar of laughter. We turned and saw Nelson Fell sprawled in a leather chair, head back, helpless to control the tears streaming down his cheeks.

I thought he had gone mad. I clutched at Chip's arm.

Nelson Fell, laughing and crying and pounding his fist against the arm of the chair all at the same time, was a frightening spectacle.

Even Mr. Thatcher, who'd spent the last ten minutes not looking at us and giving the impression of a man who would rather be anywhere else but where he was, couldn't help staring at the crazed giant.

Chip snatched up the transcript from where it had fallen on the floor and gave it to Mr. Bauer without a word.

The principal read it, frowned, and looked over at Mr. Fell, who was still convulsed. Mr. Bauer read it again. He put it down on his desk and folded his hands. He seemed not to know what to do next.

Mr. Fell finally dried his eyes and sat forward in the chair.

"Where," he gasped, "did you get that?"

"I can't tell you that," Chip repeated stubbornly. "I'm sorry, Mr. Fell, but I think you have a lot more explaining to do than we have. Everyone around here," he looked pointedly at Mr. Bauer, "is blaming the messenger for the message. All we did is report what happened — but you're the one who made it happen."

"I owe you no explanation. You sneaked around and spied on me or tapped my phone — "

"We did *not* tap your phone."

"And used your 'evidence' to libel me."

Chip started to protest again.

"I said, *libel me.* Because that's what you did. And you're going to print a retraction and explain this to the school board in person if necessary, or I'll slap a lawsuit on your parents that'll make your head spin. Now I'm going to explain to you what you *thought* you heard. And let me tell you something. The only reason I'm explaining this to you at all is because I want the satisfaction of seeing the look on your face when you find out what a damned jackass you are."

For the first time Chip seemed to lose some of his composure.

I thought Mr. Fell might be stalling for time, building up this long introduction while he was trying to think of some explanation for his telephone conversation.

I hoped so, because it suddenly flashed through my mind that while Chip was so gallantly protecting me, it was entirely my fault that there was any "evidence" at all.

"Have you ever," began Mr. Fell, "heard of the commodities market?"

Blank. It sounded sort of familiar, but I didn't know what it was. Chip, however, probably did. Because when I turned to give him an inquiring look, his face was white as a sheet.

"I see you've heard of it," Mr. Fell said. He sounded almost sadistically pleased. "You know then that it's somewhat like the stock market, except that you buy futures instead of shares of stock and these futures are for commodities instead of companies. Commodities like sugar, soybeans, cattle — called 'live beef' — and *hogs*."

Mr. Bauer had a hand clamped to his forehead. Mr. Thatcher simply looked dazed. I felt like I was lost on the Yellow Brick Road and nothing made any sense.

"Douglas Denton is my broker," Mr. Fell continued.

"What you call your 'evidence' — what you eavesdropped on, was a conversation in which he suggested I sell my beef futures and buy hog futures."

My knees finally buckled. I fell into the chair in front of Mr. Bauer's desk and went utterly numb. I don't know what happened for the next few minutes because I didn't hear anything. All I could hear was a voice in my mind, repeating over and over again, "What have I done? What have I done? What have I *done?*"

The next thing I knew, the voice was coming out of my mouth and it was saying, "Don't blame Chip. It's all my fault. I bugged your office."

"Carrie!" Chip's voice was a howl of despair.

How nice, I thought dully. He still cares. Perhaps they will let him come to see me on visiting days.

⦃XIV⦄

I don't remember too much about the next half hour or so.

When somebody lectures you at the top of his lungs for that long a time, you tend to tune out after the first few minutes and let your mind wander to pleasanter things, happier times. At least, I do. From where I was sitting, in front of Mr. Bauer's desk, I could see out his window without him realizing that I was not looking at him while he yelled.

It was interesting. There were quite a few people out there milling around the flagpole. I didn't know who they were or why they were milling around the flagpole like that. I could see they weren't kids though. So I pondered that for a while.

I have sort of a hazy memory of Chip insisting that he was responsible for what went into the lunchroom story, because he was the one who had jumped to the wrong conclusion, even if I was the person who had bugged Mr. Fell. He also said something about everyone zeroing in on this one mistake so they could ignore all the rest of the charges in the story.

Mr. Fell demanded to know where Chip had gotten the evidence for the other charges, and Chip naturally refused to reveal his source.

They talked about a retraction, which Chip would write and which would be mimeographed and distributed tomorrow. Mr. Bauer lectured me on electronic eavesdropping, invasion of privacy, and general sneakiness. He lectured both of us on responsible journalism, getting your facts straight, and the difference between freedom of speech and license to libel.

On and on it went, until I finally realized that this was all Mr. Bauer was going to do to me. I suspect that the reason nothing worse than a stern talking-to was my punishment wasn't because I was Dr. Wasserman's little girl, but because Mr. Bauer simply couldn't think of anything terrible enough to punish me with.

At last Mr. Bauer's phone rang, breaking the rhythm of his speech.

When he hung up he looked grim. "It seems," he announced, "that the cafeteria is full of students waiting for their lunch, but there is no lunch. The staff has walked out."

"Walked out?" Mr. Fell repeated. "Walked out *where?*"

For the first time that morning Mr. Thatcher said something. He pointed at the people around the flagpole and said, "Out there, I think."

So that's who all those people were! Mr. Bauer and Mr. Fell stared out the window at the crowd and groaned.

"I'd better talk to them," said Mr. Fell. He glowered at Chip. "I have a pretty good idea of what's upset them."

Mr. Bauer stood up. "I'll go with you. And I'll see *you* at three o'clock."

He ushered us out of his office and he and Mr. Fell hurried off to talk to the cafeteria staff.

Chip turned to Mr. Thatcher and said, "I don't know why you were there. You didn't know a thing about this."

"That's why I was there."

Chip looked puzzled for a moment. Then he nodded. "Oh, yeah, I see what you mean. But he didn't even say anything to you."

"He said quite a bit before you got here." Mr. Thatcher was very subdued. "And he's not finished yet. He's still deciding whether there's going to be a paper at Lincoln this year, whether you're going to be allowed to edit it if there is, and who's going to be your adviser if they do let you continue publishing."

Chip looked as if he were going to be sick.

I felt my head spinning. The only thing I could think of to say was, "Does that mean you won't be our adviser anymore?"

He shrugged. "I don't know. They don't think I did a very good job so far. If you take my advice, you'll write a humble apology as a retraction and act as meek as you can this afternoon, no matter what Mr. Bauer says."

Chip glared at Mark Thatcher. Humble and meek are not Chip's image — not as editor of the *Log*, and certainly not as crusading reporter.

"Instead of attacking me and the paper," Chip said angrily, "they ought to be cleaning up their own act. Just because we made one minor error in our story — "

"It wasn't a minor error, it was a major error, and it makes all the rest of your charges suspect. Anyway, Fell said he would investigate the other charges you made."

"That's like the fox guarding the henhouse," Chip muttered.

"Look," Mr. Thatcher said mildly, "I'm suggesting, that's all. You don't have to do anything you don't want to. But if you want to stay on as editor of the paper — if you want Lincoln to have a paper at all, I think the best way to deal with the administration is to admit your mistake and let them see you'll do everything in your power to correct it and make up for it."

We got passes from a secretary and Chip walked me to the gym. I was still wearing my ugly gym suit, of course, but it seemed awfully unimportant now. Chip was in a black mood. I thought that the only reason he walked with me was because he needed someone to listen to him arguing with himself.

"What I should do is resign," he said. "I should stick to my principles and resign. You can't have a free press if you have to cater to special-interest groups. I am *not* going to pretend we have freedom of speech when we really don't."

"That would be hypocritical," I agreed. Even in my gym suit, even with Chip in a deep funk, it was wonderful to be near him like this, and to have him talk to me again. I could almost forget the awfulness of the last hour and the awfulness to come this afternoon. Listening to Chip reveal his innermost feelings — to me, to *me*, not to Prudie! — made me nearly light-hearted.

The fact that those feelings were mostly doubt and misery didn't mar my happiness. Quite the opposite. After all, you'll tell *anyone* how happy you are. You're much more selective about whom you share your pain with.

"On the other hand," Chip said, "we were wrong. *I* was wrong. I do owe Fell a retraction. And Mark is right when he said that one mistake tends to weaken your whole story. If you make one mistake you might have made ten mistakes. I really did jump to wild conclusions without enough evidence."

"Well, it was my fault," I said. "If I hadn't given you that tape, none of this would have happened."

"But I'm responsible for everything that goes in that paper. Maybe I should resign to save myself from being canned. Maybe I should resign because I'm not a good editor."

We were at the doors to the gym. "You're a very good editor," I said softly, "and you know it. We made one mistake. We'll make up for it. I think you'd be very unhappy if you stopped being editor of the *Log*."

He smiled ruefully. "You're right about that."

I waited for a moment, hoping he would say something

else. Something like, "Carrie, it's good to talk to you. No one else understands me like you do. I could never say these things to Prudie."

But all he said was, "See you later."

When I walked into the Log office that afternoon everyone was there except Peter and Prudie. Papers were piled all over the place. Cindy was looking frantic. She had a ruler in one hand and her calculator in the other. She was running from table to table measuring stacks of papers, then figuring out something on the calculator.

"We've still only got about five hundred," she wailed. "No matter how many times I check it it always comes out the same."

She dropped into a chair, exhausted.

"Five hundred and twenty-eight," I said, dropping the copies I had managed to collect onto a desk.

"I'm surprised we got that many back," said Bob.

Chip was in the rear of the room, typing up something. His retraction, I guessed.

Peter lurched into the office. He looked scared.

He headed straight for me and asked, "What happened after we left? I've been so *nervous*."

"Don't worry," I said. "Your secret is safe with me. No, really, they don't know a thing. Your name never came up. And it won't, I promise. I told them I did it, so they figure they have the culprit." I shrugged. "And they do. They never thought to ask if I had an accessory."

He breathed a deep sigh of relief. "Thank you," he said fervently. "*Thank you*." His face clouded for a moment.

"I — uh — in all the excitement I forgot to ask you. Did I — um — I mean, at the dinner Saturday night — I think I might have —" He seemed very uncomfortable.

"Let's not even talk about that. I made a horrible fool of myself. But in all this uproar it just doesn't seem that important anymore."

"No." His face slowly brightened. "No, I guess it doesn't. It's an ill wind that doesn't blow anybody any good."

And behind every silver lining there's a cloud.

The door opened again and Mr. Bauer entered. There was dead silence as he looked around the room.

"How many copies did you get back?" he asked bluntly.

Cindy hesitated. "Five hundred."

"Then there are five hundred still in the hands of students."

She nodded. "We did our best, Mr. Bauer. Every one of us has been to every room in this school at least twice. We had people near lockers to catch the kids on their way home. A lot of kids said they threw the paper out already. We didn't know what else to do. We couldn't search them or beat them up."

His face was grim.

Chip walked slowly to the front of the room and handed the principal a piece of paper.

"This is the retraction you asked for. I did it on a stencil and they can run it off tomorrow morning and everyone will have a copy tomorrow afternoon in homeroom. Also I thought we might put out a special one-page issue of the *Log*, so the retraction gets the same prominence the original story did. That'll take two weeks though. And we'll have to take the money for it out of our yearly budget, so we'll probably have to publish one less issue."

Mr. Bauer seemed a little surprised at Chip's attitude, which certainly seemed to have changed since this morning. He gave Chip back the stencil. "It's a start," he said. He looked around. "Is everyone here?"

Chip frowned. Prudie isn't here, I thought. Where *was* Prudie? The principal had expressly ordered everyone to be at this meeting and everyone was — except for her.

"We're all here," Chip said at last.

"All right then. Many of you are aware of the trouble that you've caused, not only by false charges against the district director of the school lunch program, but by unsubstantiated claims of dishonesty on the part of the cafeteria staff."

Chip looked like he desperately wanted to say something, but he clamped his lips together in a narrow line and kept his mouth firmly shut.

"The reason many of you didn't get lunch today was because the staff walked out in protest over your accusations. The union representative was ready to call a full-fledged strike over this issue. . . ."

He went on for a long time. Responsibility to our school; a student newspaper being a privilege, not a right; libel laws; irresponsible accusations; Mr. Bauer's private debate with himself about how to deal with us, etc., etc. How many times, and in how many different ways, did he want us to apologize, I wondered? And why didn't he get to what I really wanted to know? Would we continue to have a school newspaper, and would Chip be allowed to edit it?

"So I've decided," he said finally, "to give you one more chance." He looked squarely at Chip. "I've spoken to Mr. Thatcher as well as to your guidance counselor and to your teachers and they all feel that this mistake in judgment on your part is not typical."

Oh, thank goodness. I sighed deeply and closed my eyes for a moment. I wondered if Chip could feel any more relieved for himself than I did.

"You're to consider yourself — all of you — and the *Log*, on probation. From now on your adviser is to read everything that goes in the *Log* before it's printed. Mr. Thatcher has agreed that this is a reasonable course to follow to prevent a repetition of this kind of incident."

Chip's face grew hard. Don't say anything, I pleaded silently. Don't louse it up now. We're almost out of it, and we're getting off *easy*.

"Beginning tomorrow," Mr. Bauer went on, "Mr. Fell is undertaking a thorough investigation of the other charges you made against the cafeteria staff. It would be a much easier investigation if you would tell him where you got your information."

Chip shook his head. "I'm sorry, but I can't do that. I made a promise that I would never tell. I can't break that promise, no matter what."

Mr. Bauer almost smiled. "I really didn't think you would — no matter what. It makes me wonder though whether you were really that concerned with performing

156

a public service by exposing people, or whether your motive was simply to write a hot story."

Chip didn't say anything for a moment. Then he replied, "Shouldn't a good journalist try to do both?"

I wanted to applaud.

Mr. Bauer left a moment later and the staff erupted in cheers. Without even thinking I ran over to Chip and threw my arms around him. "You were *fantastic!*" I cried. "You were *perfect.*"

Everyone gathered around him, babbling at once. As soon as I realized that I was hugging him, I dropped my arms and stood back. Everyone wanted to hug him or pound him on the shoulder or shake his hand. We were almost hysterical with relief.

But Chip looked distracted, depressed. He wasn't elated at all. Mr. Thatcher had sold out by promising to read all our copy, which was against his principles. Maybe Chip felt that by staying on as editor of the *Log* under the conditions Mr. Bauer demanded, he was selling out too.

What difference did it make? I wanted to shout. You're still the editor of the *Log,* there still *is* a *Log* and that's all that counts.

Now Chip was looking around, over the heads of people, searching the room as if for someone hidden behind a desk. He nodded absently when people spoke to him, as if he wasn't really listening.

He wasn't depressed by knuckling under to the administration, I realized. He wasn't distracted by thoughts of principle *or* principal.

He was wondering where Prudie Tuckerman was.

{XV}

I didn't exactly sneak into the house when I got home that afternoon, but neither did I yell, "Hey, it's me!" when I eased the front door open and shut it very softly behind me. I may have been tiptoeing as I headed toward the stairs but it didn't matter. My father caught me before I had my foot on the first step.

"Well," said Dr. Wasserman, the child psychologist, "if it isn't my daughter the spy."

My father's primary rule for dealing with kids is, "Criticize the behavior, not the person." I had a feeling he had forgotten about being a psychologist and was going to act like a father.

"They told you?"

"Of course they told me. Did you think they wouldn't?"

I was *hoping* they wouldn't. I didn't say anything. I suspected that anything I said would just make it worse. My father's face already looked like a thundercloud and he hadn't even gotten warmed up yet.

"How could you do such a thing? The President of the United States has to get a court order before he can tap someone's phone, but a little thing like illegal invasion of privacy doesn't stop *you*."

"I didn't tap his phone," I said timidly.

"Don't split hairs with me!" he roared.

I wondered where my mother was. Why wasn't she here, either yelling at me along with him, or sticking up for me?

My father spoke — spoke is not exactly the right word — for quite a while. He asked if I realized the position I put him in. I said I did now, but hadn't realized it when I got the idea to bug Mr. Fell. I said that when I'd started at Lincoln he'd told me I had to live my own school life and forget he was my father.

So he did a quick about-face and said it didn't matter what his position was at school, *any* father would be upset by what I had done.

At one point, Jen came in from the kitchen to the hall, where we were still standing, and said, "I think what Carrie did is neat. And *brave*."

"You're confusing brave with stupid," my father retorted. "And this doesn't concern you anyway. Go to your room."

"Why should I go to my room? I'm not the one you're mad at."

"That's only a matter of time," my father said menacingly. "Now get out of here!"

She got out of there. But I didn't. Not for a good, long time.

I found out later from Jen that my parents had had a big discussion about me before I got home and my mother was very upset with my father for being so upset about me. She was holding out for the "youthful mistake" attitude and felt that he was overreacting because of his job at school. She said it would be unfair to penalize me any more than if he didn't work at the same school I went to; and he said that she didn't understand how embarrassing this was for him.

From what Jen could overhear (Jen is really far more experienced in eavesdropping than I am), my mother finally decided that the problem was between my father and me and she would just abstain.

I thought that was kind of a cop-out on her part and really resented her not sticking up for what she believed, for my sake — but at least she acted normal to me for the next few days, while my father alternated between cold stares and sarcastic remarks.

If things were sticky at home that week, they were downright unreal at school.

Events in the next four days crowded together so crazily that I was too stunned and confused to sort them out until much later. It was the weirdest ninety-six hours of my life.

On Tuesday afternoon Chip, Jessie, Bob, and I were in the *Log* office, working on the special one-page issue of the *Log* that Chip had promised would follow the mimeographed retraction.

Prudie sashayed into the office, treated us all to a syrupy smile, and perched on the desk where Chip was working.

"Hah they-ah. What's happenin'?"

Chip stared at her as if he couldn't believe what he was seeing.

"If you were here yesterday," he said, "you'd know what was happening. Where were you yesterday afternoon, Prudie?"

"Whah, Ah was home." She put one finger on his sleeve and traced the pattern of his shirt. Her eyes were wide and innocent.

Chip pushed his chair back and stood up, so he was out of reach of Prudie's magic fingers. "And why were you home? You heard Bauer tell us all to be here. Everyone was here, Prudie. Everyone whose name is on the masthead of the *Log*. Even our typists were here. Why weren't you?"

My heart began to hammer wildly. Chip was angry at Prudie! Chip was yelling at Prudie! I knew instinctively that Prudie was not used to being yelled at. By anyone — but especially not by males. And I knew, with the same instinct, that Prudie was not going to stand for it. Jessie was looking at me. It was all I could do to keep from jumping up and down and crying, "Oh boy! Oh boy!"

"Whah, what in the world should Ah be heah foah? Ah didn't have anything to do with that story."

"Neither did Bob. Neither did Cindy. Neither did our five typists, because I typed it myself. But *they* were here."

"Well Ah just didn't see the point in sittin' heah and gettin' a dull old lectuah foah somethin' that wasn't mah fault."

"There's such a thing as loyalty, Prudie," Chip said slowly. "Loyalty is sticking with your friends when there's trouble."

"Ah believe Ah know the definition of loyalty." Prudie's voice was like ice. She got down off her perch on the desk.

"I believe you don't," Chip said quietly.

Prudie stared at him for a moment. "Does that mean you don't want me on youah precious little pay-pah anymoah?" She sounded positively threatening. I knew what she meant behind the words she was saying, and I was sure Chip knew too. She was not only leaving the *Log*, but leaving him. She didn't care all that much about the *Log* anyhow; she never had. But if Chip had spoken to her in private, she might have been able to fix things up between them. By scolding her like a naughty child in front of everyone, he'd almost forced her to quit in a snit.

And calling the *Log* Chip's "precious little paper" wasn't going to do much to soften Chip's attitude toward her.

I waited, almost not breathing, for one of them to try and save the situation. All Prudie had to do was apologize. All Chip had to do was let her stay on the paper and excuse her "disloyalty" by chalking it up to inexperience.

"Well?" demanded Prudie. "Ah'm waitin' foah youah decision, Chip."

"I think," said Chip slowly, "*you* made the decision. Yesterday afternoon."

And with that, Prudie Tuckerman whirled around and stalked out of the *Log* office and out of my life.

I jumped up, wanting to race over to Chip and throw my arms around him. But Jessie caught me by the wrist and shook her head. "Give him some time," she whispered. "He's going to need it. And take my advice — don't say a word about her."

She was right, of course. But I could hardly contain myself. The virus had passed. Chip was cured. Well, maybe not cured, but at least on the road to recovery. He had seen through Prudie, seen her for what she really was. It had to be only a matter of time till he came back to me.

"Well," said Bob, breaking the hushed silence that followed Prudie's exit, "gone with the wind."

I giggled.

Chip didn't.

On Wednesday, during last period, Chip and I were summoned to Mr. Bauer's office again. When they called me out of Social Studies, I was in an absolute panic. I didn't realize Chip had been sent for too, until I got to the office and found him waiting in front of the principal's door.

I didn't even have time to ask if he knew what was going on. As soon as I arrived, Mr. Bauer opened the door and motioned for us to come in. He wasn't alone. Nelson Fell was there too.

"We thought you'd want to know," said Mr. Bauer, "the results of Mr. Fell's investigation of your charges."

"That was a fast investigation," muttered Chip.

"It was fast because it was easy," Mr. Fell said. "If you had been a little more thorough you would have found out the real facts in this case."

"I thought I had," said Chip, "or I wouldn't have printed them."

"It was really very simple." Mr. Fell looked a lot like a TV detective explaining his discovery of who the murderer is. He had that kind of a smug smile on his face and was tapping his fingertips together. It may have annoyed Chip, but to me it was a relief to see Mr. Fell smiling instead of turning purple.

"The first thing I did was check to see if anyone on the staff had received a termination notice."

"A what?" asked Chip.

"A notice that you're being fired. And I found out that someone had. Although the notice had only gone out last week, this person was well aware that he was about to be fired because of several warnings he'd gotten already. So I spoke to some members of the cafeteria staff and found that this person was considered a troublemaker, a liar, and probably a thief. At the very least, he wasn't doing his job. Even his union didn't want to back him up, and his union representative told him so."

I glanced at Chip to see if he understood what Mr. Fell was getting at, because I didn't. Chip's face was grim.

"After that," Mr. Fell continued, "I had a little talk with the person in question. He freely admitted that he was your informant; he was rather proud of himself. He actually seemed to be enjoying all the trouble he'd stirred up."

"But that doesn't mean," I said timidly, "that what he told Chip wasn't true. I mean, just because nobody liked him and he was fired."

"Except," said Mr. Fell, "that he told me he made up every single accusation that you printed as fact in that story."

Chip went pale. "Every single one?" he choked. "All of them? Lies?"

"That's right. He said this was his perfect opportunity to get back at the whole bunch of them, and he was glad he did it. He knew nobody liked him. He considered this his revenge."

"But the short deliveries on milk." Chip's voice sounded strangled. "I saw that for myself. I even counted the containers myself one day when the delivery came in."

"But who told you how many there were *supposed* to be?" Mr. Fell had a really smarmy look on his face. He was having a good time.

Chip groaned. "Cottage Cheese," he muttered.

"What?" asked Mr. Bauer.

"Nothing," said Chip dully.

"But why did he admit it?" I asked. "Everyone would be in more trouble if he insisted he was telling the truth."

"No, they wouldn't have. Because the charges just wouldn't stand up. They were too easily checked out. And he knew that. All you had to do was come to me and ask me how many cartons of milk are delivered each day and that lie would have been exposed."

Chip looked sick.

"So your informant, for his own perverse reasons, was proud of himself for getting even with everyone he hated. He wanted to tell someone about his triumph. I happened to be the one who asked him."

Oh, poor Chip. He was wiped out.

It was agreed that another mimeographed retraction would be circulated tomorrow, this one clearing the whole cafeteria staff and the dairy company of all the charges made against them in the *Log*. The special issue of the *Log* would explain in detail the mistakes we'd made in our investigation of both Mr. Fell and the lunchroom employees.

I practically had to lead Chip out of the office as if I was his guide dog. My heart ached for him. I felt helpless in the face of his misery. All I could do was listen to him mumble, over and over again, "I made a fool of myself. I made a *fool* of myself. How could I have been so stupid?"

That afternoon, while Chip typed up his second retraction on a stencil, I sat quietly in the *Log* office, just in case he needed some help.

At least, I told myself that's why I was there.

We were the only ones in the office and I didn't say a word to him as he worked. I just watched him, hunched at the typewriter, depression hovering over him like a dark cloud.

166

Finally he sighed and pulled the Ditto master out of the typewriter. He looked up and seemed startled to see me.

"Oh, Carrie, are you still here?"

I nodded. "Still here." Like a faithful pet.

"You want a ride home?" he asked. "I'm finished here."

Do I want a ride home? Is the sky blue? Does a duck quack? Will I fail Geometry? Yesyesyesyesyes!

"That would be nice."

Chip was so depressed as he drove to my house that when we got there, I worked up my courage and asked him to come in. I wanted so badly to help him, to have him talk to me, to let me reassure him — but he wouldn't get out of the car. I think he was afraid to face my father. (Why not? *I* still was.)

If all this hadn't happened, I think Chip might have been able to work out some of his confusion and disappointment over Prudie, but being so involved with the disaster of the *Log*, he probably had had no time to sort out his emotional life.

I sighed. I thanked him for the lift home and resigned myself to waiting.

When the phone rang that night I leaped for it. Maybe it would be Chip, calling to —

"Do you know," Terry demanded, "what that big oaf has done?"

"Don't you say hello anymore?" I asked dejectedly. "And to which big oaf are you referring?"

"Marty."

"Oh, *that* big oaf."

"He is making a complete jerk of himself. Someone ought to tell him."

"I hope you weren't expecting *me* to," I said. "How is he making a complete jerk of himself?"

"He is utterly infatuated with a brainless flirt named — get this — Prudie Tuckerman."

I was staggered. "Boy, that girl works fast!"

"What do you mean?"

"Well, up until yesterday she had Chip slobbering all over her. How did she get to Marty so fast?"

"Yesterday? Tuesday? But she was there at football practice Monday waiting for him. I saw her."

"Monday?" I echoed. "Monday afternoon?" That was when she didn't show up at the *Log* meeting Mr. Bauer had called.

Holy cow. For Prudie, there would always be plenty of fish in the sea. Sometimes, even plenty of fish on one line. Boy, wait till I tell Chip!

I could call him and say, "Oh, by the way, Chip, Prudie was *not* home Monday afternoon. A reliable source told me —" No. It was not the thing to do. And we'd all had enough of "reliable sources."

"He's following her around all over the place, meeting her between classes, waiting by her locker. It's *disgusting*."

"How do you know all this?" I asked curiously.

"I saw him. And so have a lot of other people. They told me."

"But what do you care, Ter? You didn't want to go with him anymore."

"It's humiliating. He certainly got over me fast. And now everybody knows it."

"He didn't get over you that fast. Besides, just how long did you want him to suffer before he got over you?"

"Longer than this," Terry snarled.

"You're acting like a dog in the manger," I said. "You're being very irrational."

She started — oh, God — to cry. "I want him back!" she wailed. "I made a mistake breaking off. Football season is practically over. Everything would have been all right."

"Oh, Terry."

I didn't even try to reason with her. I just waited until she was finished crying, then said something comforting and hung up.

Why, I wondered, as I lay in the dark trying to sleep, do people always seem to want the person they haven't got, or can't get? Even I, who was so devoted to Chip, toyed with having crushes on Mr. Sachs and Mr. Thatcher. Was that because they were so completely unattainable? Because I knew I could never get romantically involved with them? Because someone you weren't sure of, or couldn't have, or who belonged to someone else, was more exciting and more desirable than someone who was available?

Have I discovered a law of human nature, I wondered?

I turned over onto my stomach.

Probably not.

{XVI}

Friday afternoon I told Chip that I was going to interview Mr. Sachs again. At least I'd be doing something, instead of sitting around like a bump in the *Log* office, as I had on Wednesday and Thursday, waiting for Chip to get over the Prudie virus.

"Again?" Chip asked.

"You mean," Bob said with a leer, "once is not enough?"

"Oh, come on," I grumbled. "You all told me how lousy the first interview was and Mr. Sachs was wondering why we didn't use it. I had to tell him we'd run it in the next issue, but we haven't got anything to run. That's why I made up a whole new list of questions to ask him."

It should take at least an hour, I thought. I allowed myself a small, delicious shiver. After all, until Chip came around — if he ever did — I was entitled to shiver over anyone I pleased.

"What an eager little beaver you are, Carrie." Bob grinned. "We haven't even gotten over the flak from the first issue yet and here you can't wait to start on the second."

Chip looked from Bob to me as if we were speaking some secret language that he didn't understand.

"Well, there's nothing like work to take your mind off disaster," I said briskly.

"And interviewing Sachs," Bob said, in a perfectly awful imitation of Groucho Marx, "is nothing like work."

"Don't be silly," I said. "It's strictly business."

"Sure it is," said Bob.

I glanced sideways at Chip and got flustered when I realized that he was glancing sideways at *me*.

I cleared my throat. "Well. I guess I'd better get going. I told Mr. Sachs I'd be there right after the last class."

"Who is this Mr. Sachs?" asked Chip finally.

"Chip, I told you. He's my Biology teacher."

"And a fine specimen he is too," said Bob. I was about ready to tell him to stuff the insinuating remarks when I noticed that Chip had a thoughtful frown on his face.

"How come," he said slowly, "you're so interested in this Sachs guy?"

For a minute I couldn't believe Chip had said that. It sounded almost as if he were . . . jealous.

No. Ridiculous. Impossible. Why should he be jealous? I'd been sitting in the *Log* office for two days waiting for him to stop mooning over the belle of the boll weevils and he'd hardly acknowledged my existence, except for two brief rides home. Why should he care who I was interested in, when he'd made it perfectly clear he wasn't the least bit interested in me?

I just stood there, staring dumbly at Chip and trying to figure out what was going on. Chip faced me, his arms folded, waiting for me to answer his question.

"Why am I so interested in Mr. Sachs?" I repeated finally. Before I could answer — not that I knew what the answer was supposed to be — Bob said, "If you'd ever seen this guy, you wouldn't have to ask why she was interested."

"Oh, stuff it," I retorted. Brilliant remark, Carrie. But I was getting irritated and impatient and time was a-wasting. Mr. Sachs was expecting me.

"I think," Chip said slowly, "I'll go along to the interview with you, Carrie. Maybe I can help you out — give you a few pointers, you know."

"I don't need any pointers," I snapped. "I have my questions all written out and —"

"Yeah, but maybe I can see where you're going wrong. I mean, you said yourself you're not too good at interviews —"

"Then let me get some practice! I don't see why you have to stand over me like I was a — a *baby* or something."

"Why are you so eager to be alone with this guy, Carrie?" Chip asked suspiciously.

"Are you *crazy*? Have you gone completely out of your gourd?" I was practically shrieking at him. What had gotten into him? What gave him the right to act like this after the way he'd treated me? Even if I did want to be alone with Mr. Sachs — and I could certainly think of a few thousand worse ways to spend an hour — what business was it of his?

He was acting just like a jealous nut.

"Look, Chip, first of all —" I stopped in midsentence.

He *is* acting like a jealous nut. Is it true? Is he actually *jealous*? Of *me and Mr. Sachs*? But that is so stupid, so impossible, and besides, what does he care who I have a crush on? He's been too busy brooding over his broken heart to pay any attention to mine.

What was it that I'd been thinking about last night, when I thought I might have discovered a law of human nature? Something about how someone you aren't sure of, or who belonged to someone else, is more desirable than someone who's available?

It's true! I realized. Chip *is* jealous! That's why he's acting like a jealous nut. Because he *is* a jealous nut.

Very swift, Caroline J. Wasserman. It certainly took you long enough to catch on. And now what? It's all so ridiculous — for Chip to be jealous of someone who there's no possibility will ever compete with him for my affections . . .

Oh, sure, I can just see it now. Chip and Mr. Sachs leaping over desks and sinks in the biology lab, swords clashing in a duel to the death.

"She'll be mine, by God!" Slash, clank.

"That's what you think! Touché, you cur!" Clang, swoosh.

I giggled. I couldn't help it.

This is all so silly. Life is so silly. Love is so silly. *Chip* is so silly!

"What's so funny?" Chip demanded.

"Not funny, silly," I replied without thinking. I wasn't going to try and figure it out now. The important thing was not to ask questions, the important thing was that Chip was *jealous!*

"Carrie." Chip's voice was gentle. "Carrie, there's something I —"

"My goodness, look at the time!" Bob said loudly. "I'd better get moving if I'm going to cover football practice." He grabbed his jacket and books and hurried out of the office, closing the door carefully behind himself.

Chip sat down on a desk and took one of my hands in both of his. He squeezed it gently and began rubbing my knuckles with his thumb. I swallowed a few times and felt my knees grow weak. There you go again, Caroline J. Wasserman. Why should your knees turn to water just because Chip is massaging your knuckles? The kneebone isn't connected to the knucklebone. The kneebone's connected to the thighbone and the thighbone's connected to the hipbone. None of them is connected to the knucklebone.

Now stop that! I told myself. Concentrate. What is Chip saying?

". . . really have been stupid. About — a lot of things. Sometimes you don't know when you have a good thing."

I stared at him. Did he mean me? Was I the good thing he didn't know he had? That *must* be what he meant. These are *my* knuckles he's rubbing, after all.

"I was — well — infatuated I guess is the only word for what I was."

Stupid is another word, I thought briefly.

"But I'm over that." He pulled me closer to him. "I learned the difference between . . . well, between someone who stands by you and really cares and someone who — who —"

Merely makes you drool, I finished. But not out loud.

I really wasn't feeling bitter, though. Not here, not like this. Standing so close to Chip, both my hands now clasped tightly in his, I was feeling glorious.

"Carrie, what I'm trying to say —" He was struggling, poor thing. Poor, darling, apologetic Chip.

"I know," I said softly. "You don't have to say it."

He seemed to relax a little. He slid off the desk and stood in front of me, looking down into my eyes. All the tension suddenly seemed to drain out of him. "That's one of the best things about you, Carrie," he said, his voice low. "You understand even when I don't say it."

I could hardly believe it. This whole scene, which I had imagined so many times, was turning out almost exactly as I'd pictured it. Chip was speaking the very lines I had written in my fantasy script.

He put his arms around me and kissed me. For a long time.

"Mr. Sachs," I finally murmured. "Mr. Sachs is waiting for me."

He kissed me again. And there went my knees again, nearly buckling under me. The lip bone isn't connected to the kneebone, I thought wildly. There isn't even such a thing as a lip bone. Lips don't have bones.

"Carrie?" Chip twined his fingers in mine and brought them to his lips. Oh, dear. I was definitely melting.

"Carrie?"

"Hmm?"

"Let him wait."